喚醒你的英文語感！

Get a Feel for English !

喚醒你的英文語感！

Get a Feel for English !

貝塔語言出版
Beta Multimedia Publishing

IRT 語言測驗中心
Language Testing Center

附一片朗讀MP3

英文閱讀越好 旅遊篇

人文、風俗、歷史、地理、建築、旅遊英文，一覽無遺！

從一生必遊的21個地理奇景，
讀出與世界接軌的**好知識** + **好英文**！

Thousands of ... Stonehenge ... least partly ...

There is a high sandstone cliff.
Carved into the cliff is a rectangular space,
like a giant door, forty meters high.

Despite the damage, the Colosseum's high curving walls and dozens of arched openings are still impressive.

Islamic features like minarets are added to Hagia Sophia, and Christian images inside the church are covered with white paint.

Neuschwanstein Castle in Germany looks just like you expect a castle to look.

For thirty-eight centuries, it was the tallest and arguably the most impressive structure on Earth. It was built to protect the dead body of one man. His name was Khufu.

作者：Jeff Hammons

序言

本書所介紹的都是著名奇景。大部分景點都是聯合國教科文組織（UNESCO）的世界遺產名單網站上所列出的建築或遺跡。它們被收錄在聯合國的名單和本書裡，因為它們是人類有史以來最驚人的成就。

諸如泰姬瑪哈陵、聖索菲亞大教堂和巴特農神廟，這些紀念性建築都是史上一些最偉大、最了不起的社會所產生的菁華。它們不僅是建築，更已成為整個文化的象徵。

並非人人都能欣賞這些遺址的價值。過去當地居民曾把圓形石林的石頭拿去蓋房子和築籬笆。在開羅的建築裡，還是可以看到鑲有一塊塊把吉薩大金字塔堆砌起來的光亮白石。羅馬競技場的大理石也被拆去蓋羅馬的教堂和其他建築。

有些遺址則是遭到想帶紀念品回家的訪客所破壞。希臘人努力了多年，要英國歸還從衛城所拆走的女像柱。2008 年，有一位芬蘭遊客被抓到，他把復島活一具摩艾的耳朵敲了一塊下來。

在原本的古世界七大奇觀中，只有一樣還保留了下來：吉薩大金字塔。其他的都已化為塵土。但舊奇觀已被新奇觀所取代。2007 年舉辦了一項世界性的民意調查，以選出新的世界七大奇觀。這七樣皆收錄在本書中，並搭配了其他十四個決賽的入圍者。

這些文章可以讓各位對這些景點有所認識。但可別就此打住，繼續多看多學。在閱讀時，別忘了如果要真正體驗及了解這些地方，坐而讀是不夠的，你還必須起而行。

有位哲學家曾經形容說，偉大的建築是凝結在空間中的音符（music frozen in space）。把造訪這些景點當成一個機會來做這件不可思議的事：欣賞凝結在空間中的音符。著手安排、做點研究、存點錢，就動身吧。

以下列出新、舊世界奇景供各位參考：

標示說明

| U | 聯合國教科文組織的世界遺產名單網站（UNESCO World Heritage Site：
http://zh.wikipedia.org/wiki/%E4%B8%96%E7%95%8C%E9%81%97%E4%BA%A7）

| O | 舊世界奇觀

| 7 | 新世界七大奇觀優勝者（前七名）

| 20 | 新世界七大奇觀決賽入圍者（前二十名）
（http://zh.wikipedia.org/wiki/%E4%B8%96%E7%95%8C%E6%96%B0%E4%B8%83%E5%A4%A7%E5%A5%87%E8%BF%B9）

非洲及阿拉伯世界

| U | O | The Great Pyramid of Giza 吉薩大金字塔

| U | 7 | Petra 佩特拉

| 20 | U | Timbuktu 廷巴克圖

亞洲和大洋洲

| 20 | U | Kiyomizu-dera 清水寺

| 20 | U | Angkor Wat 吳哥窟

| 7 | U | The Great Wall 長城

| 20 | U | Red Square 紅場

20 U Hagia Sophia 聖索菲亞大教堂
7 U The Taj Mahal 泰姬瑪哈陵
20 U The Sydney Opera House 雪梨歌劇院

歐洲

7 U The Colosseum 羅馬競技場
20 U The Acropolis 衛城
20 U The Alhambra 阿蘭布拉宮
20 The Eiffel Tower 艾菲爾鐵塔
20 Neuschwanstein 新天鵝堡
20 U Stonehenge 圓形石林

北美洲

7 U Chichén Itzá 奇琴伊察
20 U The Statue of Liberty 自由女神像

南美洲

7 U Machu Picchu 馬丘比丘
20 The Moai of Rapa Nui 拉帕努伊的摩艾
7 Christ the Redeemer 救世基督像

CONTENTS 目錄

Part 3 歐洲

Part 4 北美洲

Part 5 南美洲

PART 1

非洲和阿拉伯世界

UNIT 1 | **The Great Pyramid of Giza**
吉薩大金字塔

Located in Egypt（埃及）

❶ The Great Pyramid of Giza, completed around 2551 BC after twenty years of labor by thousands of workers, is a tomb. For thirty-eight centuries, it was the tallest and arguably[1] the most impressive structure on Earth. It was built to protect the dead body of one man. His name was Khufu.

❷ Who was Khufu and what did he do to deserve such a big tomb? Khufu, also known as Cheops, was a pharaoh.[2] He ruled ancient Egypt during the years 2589 to 2566 BC. It was a big job. Khufu had lots of power and lots of responsibilities. Then he died.

❸ When you're dead, are you done? Not according to the ancient Egyptians. They believed in life after death. But crossing over to the afterlife[3] was not an easy process. For starters, the body had to be preserved.[4] Poor Egyptians had

themselves buried in the sand and hoped for the best. Rich Egyptians spared[5] no expense. They had themselves mummified.[6]

❹ Special workers made the mummies.[7] They knew how to use a hook[8]

Ⓦ Ⓞ Ⓡ Ⓓ Ⓛ Ⓘ Ⓢ Ⓣ

1. arguably〔ˋɑrgjʊəblɪ〕*adv.* 大概（不會錯）；（充分）可以論證
2. pharaoh〔ˋfɛro〕*n.* 法老（古埃及王的尊稱）
3. afterlife〔ˋæftɚˏlaɪv〕*n.* 來世；死後的生命
4. preserve〔prɪˋzɝv〕*v.* 保存；維持
5. spare〔spɛr〕*v.* 吝惜；節省使用
6. mummify〔ˋmʌmɪˏfaɪ〕*v.* 使……成為木乃伊；使……乾枯

to remove the brain through the nose. Brains got thrown away—the ancient Egyptians figured they were a waste of space. Other organs were salted and stored in special jars. The heart was more important. Considered the source of emotion and wisdom, it was left in the body. After the body dried out, it was treated with special oils and wrapped in cloth. Rich

Egyptians built special tombs to protect their mummies. Everything that might come in handy[9] in the afterlife—food, furniture, salted organs, games—was placed in the tomb.

❺ For his tomb, Khufu built the Great Pyramid of Giza. His pyramid was the biggest of the big, bigger even than his father Sneferu's pyramid, if only by ten meters (you can be sure that was intentional). Polished[10] white stones covered the entire pyramid. It was spectacular.[11]

7. mummy〔ˋmʌmɪ〕 *n.* 木乃伊
8. hook〔hʊk〕 *n.* 鉤
9. handy〔ˋhændɪ〕 *adj.* 方便的；馬上可使用的
10. polished〔ˋpɑlɪʃt〕 *adj.* 磨光的；擦亮的
11. spectacular〔spɛkˋtækjələ〕 *adj.* 壯觀的

6 Everything up until that point—building the tomb, the funeral, mummification,[12] even *life itself*—all led up to the next and most important step. After an Egyptian mummy was sealed[13] within its tomb, Osiris, the god of the dead, appeared with 43 helpers. It was time for the ceremony of judgment known as the Weighing of the Heart. Osiris weighed the heart on a scale.[14] If the heart was pure and light—if it balanced against a feather—then Osiris opened the way to the afterlife. But if the heart was not pure—if it was heavy with the weight of bad deeds—then the demon[15] Ammit would come. Ammit had the head of a crocodile. It was her job to eat impure[16] hearts.

7 Nobody knows what happened to Khufu's heart. His mummy has never been found.

W O R D   L I S T

12. mummification〔ˌmʌməfəˋkeʃən〕 *n.* 做成木乃伊
13. seal〔sil〕 *v.* 密封；封閉
14. scale〔skel〕 *n.* 天平；秤
15. demon〔ˋdimən〕 *n.* 惡魔；鬼
16. impure〔ɪmˋpjʊr〕 *adj.* 不潔的；不純的

譯文

❶ 吉薩大金字塔是個墓地。它耗費數萬個工人 20 年的勞力，在西元前 2551 年左右完成。長達 38 個世紀的時間，它都是地球上最高、而且大概是最讓人印象深刻的結構體。它是蓋來保護一個人的屍體，他的名字叫做古夫。

❷ 誰是古夫？他有什麼功績而值得葬在這麼大的墓地裡？古夫又名基奧普斯，是一位法老。他在西元前 2589 到 2566 年間統治古埃及，這是個重大任務。古夫擁有眾多的權力與眾多的責任。後來他過世了。

❸ 死了以後，你就一了百了了嗎？古埃及人可不這麼想。他們相信來生，但跨越到來生並非簡單的過程。首先，大體必須好好保存。貧窮的埃及人會把自己葬在沙裡，並懷抱著希望。有錢的埃及人則會不惜重金，把自己做成木乃伊。

❹ 木乃伊是由特殊的工人來製作。他們懂得要怎麼用鉤子把腦漿從鼻子裡抽出來。腦漿會被丟掉——古埃及人認為，它是在浪費空間。其他的器官則會被醃放在特殊的罈子裡。心臟較為重要。它被認為是情感與智慧的源頭，所以留在身體裡。大體變乾後，會塗上特殊的油，並用布包起來。有錢的埃及人會建造特殊的墓地來保護木乃伊，並把來生可能會用到的一切放進墓地裡，像是食物、家具、醃過的器官、遊戲器材。

❺ 為了自己的墓地，古夫建造了吉薩大金字塔。他的金字塔大得不得了，甚至比他父親斯奈夫魯的金字塔還大，儘管只大了十公尺（你可以肯定那是故意的）。光亮的白色石頭蓋住整座金字塔，頗為壯觀。

❻ 到這個階段為止，建造墓地、葬禮、做成木乃伊，甚至是生命本身，一切

都是為了進入下一個最重要的步驟。當埃及木乃伊封進墓地後，死神俄賽里斯會帶著 43 個助手現身。而被稱為「秤心」的審判儀式也就在此時發生。俄賽里斯會用天平來秤心。假如心又純又輕，跟羽毛等重，俄賽里斯就會開啓通往來生的道路。但要是心「不」純，也就是重量跟惡行一樣重，惡魔阿米特就會出現。阿米特有個鱷魚頭，她的任務就是吃掉不純的心。

❼ 沒有人知道古夫的心下場如何。他的木乃伊從未被尋獲。

精要句型

■ **Crossing over to the afterlife was not an easy process. *For starters*, the body had to be preserved.**
跨越到來生並非簡單的過程。首先,大體必須保存好。

句型 **For starters, ...** 「首先,……。」

For starters 意指「一開始」或「第一步」。當你想要表示有很多事要做,而這件事只是開頭時,它就非常好用。

例句 If you want to be my boyfriend, you need to improve yourself—a lot. *For starters*, you need to get a job.
假如你想當我男朋友,你就要有所長進,而且要大大長進。首先,你得找個工作才行。

Before I can go to Egypt, I have so much to do! *For starters*, I want to learn to read ancient Egyptian hieroglyphics.
在我可以去埃及前,我有一大堆事要做!首先,我想學會看古埃及的象形文字。

詞彙測驗

( ) **1.** Which of the following definitions of **point** describes how the word is used in paragraph 6, line 1?

A. the sharp end of an object

B. the reason for doing some activity

C. a moment in time

D. a special quality or characteristic

(   ) **2.** Which of the following definitions of **appear** describes how the word is used in paragraph 6, line 4?

      A. to seem to be

      B. to present oneself before an authority

      C. to act in a play or movie

      D. to come into view

(   ) **3.** Which of the following definitions of **scale** describes how the word is used in paragraph 6, line 6?

      A. an instrument for measuring mass

      B. to climb using a ladder

      C. a series of musical notes

      D. a hard flake from a fish's skin

旅 遊 一 點 通

很多人去參觀吉薩金字塔時，都要想騎駱駝。如果你也想的話，那可要小心。駱駝有時候會對不喜歡的人吐口水。當牠們吐口水時，所吐出來的其實是唾液加上其中一個胃裡消化到一半的食物。所以，與其說是吐口水，牠比較像是在對你嘔吐，所以要小心。到下列網站看看遊客的說法，了解一下你在吉薩的駱駝身上會碰到的其他問題：

http://www.virtualtourist.com/travel/Africa/Egypt/Muhafazat_al_Qahirah/Cairo-2008750/Tourist_Traps-Cairo-Camels-BR-1.html

旅遊好用句

假如你想要跟駱駝拍照，要先問問飼主：

Excuse me. Do you mind if I take a picture of your camel?

「請問一下，你介意我跟你的駱駝拍張照嗎？」

解答

詞彙測驗

1. 在「point」的下列定義中，哪一個是在描述這個字在第六段第一行中的用法？

A. 物體的尖端

B. 做某事的原因

C. 某個時刻

D. 特質或特徵

Ans C

2. 在「appear」的下列定義中，哪一個是在描述這個字在第六段第四行中的用法？

A. 似乎

B. 出現在權威之前（出庭）

C. 演出戲劇或電影

D. 現身

Ans D

3. 在「scale」的下列定義中，哪一個是在描述這個字在第六段第六行中的用法？

A. 測量質量的儀器

B. 用梯子攀爬

C. 一連串的音符

D. 魚皮的鱗片

Ans A

UNIT 2 | Petra 佩特拉

Located in Jordan（約旦）

❶ The path is narrow, only three steps wide in places. Steep rock walls rise up more than a hundred meters on each side. The blue of the sky is visible only as a thin ribbon, high overhead. You're in The Shaft. In Arabic, it's called al-Siq. It's a deep ravine[1] in the Negev Desert in southern Jordan that twists[2] and turns through the rock for a kilometer and a half until it reaches the ancient city of Petra.

❷ The Siq opens up into a narrow valley. There is a high sandstone[3] cliff. Carved[4] into the cliff is a rectangular[5] space, like a giant door, forty meters high. Within this rectangular opening, carved from the rock like a sculpture,[6] is an amazing building: Al Khazneh (The Treasury). In the desert light, the sandstone columns and statues glow with a soft reddish[7] color. In Greek petra means rock, and many of Petra's buildings, like Al Khazneh, are carved directly from the

Ⓦ Ⓞ Ⓡ Ⓓ Ⓛ Ⓘ Ⓢ Ⓣ

1. ravine〔rəˋvɪn〕 *n.* 峽谷；深谷
2. twist〔twɪst〕 *v.* 曲折；彎曲
3. sandstone〔ˋsændˌston〕 *n.* 沙岩
4. carve〔kɑrv〕 *v.* 刻
5. rectangular〔rɛkˋtæŋgjələ〕 *adj.* 長方形的
6. sculpture〔ˋskʌlptʃə〕 *n.* 雕刻；雕像
7. reddish〔ˋrɛdɪʃ〕 *adj.* 微紅色的；略帶紅色的

rose-colored rock.

❸ Emerging[8] from the Siq, you may feel like the first person to discover the lost city of Petra. At the same time, if you watch many movies, it's probably going to look rather familiar. The exotic[9] setting and Petra's amazing, sculpted buildings have been irresistible[10] to film directors. *Mortal Kombat* happened at Petra. Indiana Jones went there looking for the Holy Grail.[11] And when the good Transformers needed to hide their Tomb of Primes from the bad Transformers, they chose Petra.

❹ The actual city of Petra was at its peak[12] from the first century BC until the third century AD. Before it was absorbed[13] into the Roman Empire, it was the capital of the Arab kingdom of Nabatea. The Nabateans were originally nomads.[14] At some point, they settled down

8. emerge〔ɪˋmɝdʒ〕 *v.* 出現
9. exotic〔ɪgˋzɑtɪk〕 *adj.* 異國情調的
10. irresistible〔͵ɪrɪˋzɪstəbḷ〕 *adj.* 不能抵抗的
11. Holy Grail〔ˋholɪ ˋgrel〕 *n.* 聖杯
12. peak〔pik〕 *n.* 高峰；頂點
13. absorb〔əbˋsɔrb〕 *v.* 併吞；吸收
14. nomad〔ˋnomæd〕 *n.* 遊牧民族

and decided to carve themselves a rock city. They picked a good place, along the trade routes that stretched from Europe to India and China. Caravans[15] of camels arrived with ivory, cloth, spices, precious stones, gold,

and exotic animals. The Nabateans got rich by taxing the caravans.

❺ Petra is in a desert and there is hardly any rain. What did the Nabateans do for water? They were clever engineers. Using dams and channels to capture[16] every drop of rain and spring water, they piped[17] it to underground reservoirs[18] away from the heat of the sun. In a place that during the entire year often gets less than 15 cm of rain, the Nabateans were able to provide water for a city with more than 20,000 residents.

❻ Walking through the Siq is like traveling back in time. Much of the city of Petra still looks like it did 2,000 years ago. Buildings carved from rock last a long time.

Ⓦ Ⓞ Ⓡ Ⓓ Ⓛ Ⓘ Ⓢ Ⓣ

15. caravan 〔ˋkærəˌvæn〕 n. （沙漠地帶的）商隊；旅行隊
16. capture 〔ˋkæptʃɚ〕 v. 擄獲；獲得
17. pipe 〔paɪp〕 v. 用管子把……輸送至
18. reservoir 〔ˋrɛzɚˌvɔr〕 n. 貯水池；水庫

譯文

❶ 路很窄，某些地方只有三步寬。兩面的陡峭石牆高達一百多公尺，湛藍的天空只能看見細絲帶般的寬度、高懸在頭頂。你所在的地方是蛇道。在阿拉伯文裡，它被稱為 al-Siq。它是約旦南部內蓋夫沙漠中的深谷，在岩石中迂迴曲折一公里半，直到抵達佩特拉古城為止。

❷ Siq 在一座狹谷展開來，那裡有一片高聳的沙岩懸崖。懸崖被切刻出一個長方形的空間，宛如一扇巨大的門，有 40 公尺高。這個長方形的開口，有如雕塑品被刻在岩石上，裡頭有一座令人讚歎的建築：艾爾卡茲尼（藏寶庫）。在沙漠的光線下，沙岩的圓柱和雕像發散出柔和的紅色光芒。在希臘文中，「佩特拉」是岩石的意思，佩特拉有很多建築都跟艾爾卡茲尼一樣，是直接從玫瑰色的岩石中切割出來。

❸ 從 Siq 走出來，你可能會覺得自己是第一個發現失落城市佩特拉的人。而且，如果你看了許多電影，八成會覺得它相當眼熟。異國風情的景色，還有佩特拉令人驚歎的雕刻建築，是電影導演無法抗拒的。《魔宮帝國》就是在佩特拉發生。印第安納‧瓊斯就是去那裡尋找聖杯。當好的變形金剛要藏好領導母體、不讓壞的變形金剛發現，選的也是佩特拉。

❹ 真實的佩特拉城是在西元前一世紀到西元三世紀達到高峰。在被羅馬帝國吞併前，它是阿拉伯王國納巴提亞的首都。納巴提亞人原本是遊牧民族。在某個時間點，他們定居下來，並決定為自己刻造一座岩城。他們沿著從歐洲延伸到印度與中國的商隊路線、挑了個好地方。駱駝車隊帶來了象牙、布匹、香料、寶石、黃金和奇特的動物。納巴提亞人靠著向車隊收費而富有了起來。

❺ 佩特拉地處沙漠，幾乎不下任何的雨。納巴提亞人用什麼方法來找水？他們是聰明的工程師。利用水壩和水道來接取每一滴雨水和泉水，他們把水導引至地下的儲水槽，以避開陽光的熱度。在一個全年雨量常常不到 15 公分的地方，納巴提亞人卻能供水給有兩萬多個居民的城市。

❻ 穿越 Siq 就像是回到過去。佩特拉城大部分看起來還是跟 2,000 年前沒兩樣。從岩石雕刻而成的建築歷久不衰。

🔑 精要句型

■ **The blue of the sky is visible *only as* a thin ribbon, high overhead.**
湛藍的天空只能看見細絲帶般的寬度、高懸在頭頂。

句型 **... only as Y.** 「……只能 Y。」

「only as」這個片語多半是用來帶出某種限制，也就是 Y。

例句 I like you, but *only as* a friend.
我喜歡你，但只能當朋友。

I'll go with you to the Taklamakan Desert, but *only as* far as Turpan—
it's too dangerous to go deeper into the desert.
我會跟你去塔克拉馬干沙漠，但最遠只能到吐魯番——再繼續往沙漠裡走就
太危險了。

✏️ 詞彙測驗

一、**Look in the essay to find the opposites of these words.**

1. wide   _____

2. modern   _____

3. entering into   _____

4. uninteresting   _____

5. find   _____

6. inept   _____

二、**Which sentence in each pair is true?**

_____ A ravine is a narrow space between two cliffs.

_____ A cliff is a narrow space between two ravines.

_____ Familiar things rarely or never seem exotic.

_____ Familiar things are always the most exotic.

_____ It takes more than one camel to make a caravan.

_____ One camel can carry many caravans.

 旅 遊 一 點 通

你可能是搭四輪的交通工具到佩特拉——而且八成是從約旦的首都安曼前往。不過，一到了現場，你就必須靠自己的雙腳來走路了。或者，也可以雇隻動物來載你。駱駝很普遍，馬和驢子也雇得到，價錢則是看你的講價能力而定。三塊錢左右的約旦幣第納爾（Jordan Dinars），大約新台幣 135 元，算是合理，但不懂阿拉伯語的遊客往往會多花錢。可以上維基旅遊網的佩特拉網頁去了解雇用駱駝、以及參觀這座岩城時所需要知道的資訊：

http://wikitravel.org/en/Petra#Get_in

旅遊好用句

雇用駱駝講價時，假裝沒興趣要離開，這一招很有用：

That's too much. Maybe I don't need a camel. Thanks anyway.
「那太貴了。也許我不需要駱駝。還是謝了。」

解 答

詞彙測驗

一、從文章中找出這些單字的反義字。

1. narrow 窄的

2. ancient 古代的

3. emerging from 從……出現

4. irresistible 無法抗拒的

5. hide 隱藏

6. clever 聰明的

二、各組句子中的哪句話是正確的？

__T__ 峽谷是兩座懸崖間的狹窄空間。

_____ 懸崖是兩座峽谷間的狹窄空間。

__T__ 熟悉的事物很少或絕對不會有異國風情。

_____ 熟悉的事物總是最有異國風情。

__T__ 需要一隻以上的駱駝才能組成商隊。

_____ 一隻駱駝就能拉很多商隊。

UNIT 3 | Timbuktu
廷巴克圖

Located in Mali（馬利，非洲西部之一共和國）

❶ Timbuktu: is it real? Or is it a mythical¹ place, like El Dorado in the Amazon jungle,² or Atlantis³ under the sea? Actually, it's both.

❷ Timbuktu is a real place. It's a town in Mali, on the southwest edge of the Sahara Desert. Around 30,000 people live there. For Africans, for hundreds of years, Timbuktu has been an important regional⁴ center for trade. Caravans⁵ from the north arrived from the desert with salt and returned with gold and slaves.

❸ Ideas also traveled with the caravans, and over time Timbuktu became an important center for Muslim⁶ scholars. There are three famous mosques⁷ in Timbuktu. The oldest, Djinguereber Mosque, was built in 1327. Sankore Mosque and Sidi Yahya Mosque are also hundreds of years old. During the 14ᵗʰ century, Sankore University had one of the largest libraries in the world. There was space for 25,000 students. They studied Islamic⁸ principles

---

ⓌⓄⓡⓓ Ⓛⓘⓢⓣ

1. mythical 〔ˋmɪθɪk!〕 *adj.* 神話的；虛構的
2. Amazon jungle 〔ˋæməˌzɑn ˋdʒʌngl〕 *n.* 亞馬遜叢林
3. Atlantis 〔ətˋlæntɪs〕 *n.* 亞特蘭提斯島
4. regional 〔ˋridʒən!〕 *adj.* 全地區內的；區域性的
5. caravan 〔ˋkærəˌvæn〕 *n.* （沙漠地帶的）商隊；旅行隊
6. Muslim 〔ˋmʌzlɪm〕 *adj.* 回教徒的
7. mosque 〔mɑsk〕 *n.* 清真寺；回教寺院
8. Islamic 〔ɪsˋlæmɪk〕 *adj.* 伊斯蘭教的；回教的

from the Koran,[9] along with subjects such as mathematics, geography, history, physics, astronomy[10] and chemistry. For Africans, Timbuktu is and has been a place for living, studying, and doing business. It's a place on the map.

❹ For Europeans, Timbuktu has always been a place off the map, a fabled[11] city, the pearl of the Sahara, the El Dorado of Africa. In 1824, the Société de Géographie in Paris offered a prize: 10,000 francs[12] to the first non-Muslim person to reach and then return alive from Timbuktu. Gordon Laing from Scotland[13] made it there in 1826, only to get killed by some locals.[14] Two years later the Frenchman René Caillié won the prize. He'd traveled to Timbuktu and back alone, disguised[15] as a Muslim.

❺ In Europe, the word Timbuktu has long been used as a metaphor.[16] When people say "Timbuktu," they mean an exotic,[17] faraway place that is hard to get to. Many Europeans and Americans still believe Timbuktu

---

9. Koran 〔ko`ræn〕 *n.* 可蘭經
10. astronomy 〔ə`strɑnəmɪ〕 *n.* 天文學
11. fabled 〔`febḷd〕 *adj.* 傳說的；捏造的
12. franc 〔fræŋk〕 *n.* 法郎
13. Scotland 〔`skɑtlənd〕 *n.* 蘇格蘭
14. local 〔`lokḷ〕 *n.* 當地居民
15. disguise 〔dɪs`gaɪz〕 *v.* 偽裝；假扮
16. metaphor 〔`mɛtəfɚ〕 *n.* 隱喻；暗喻
17. exotic 〔ɪg`zɑtɪk〕 *adj.* 異國情調的；外來的

is a legend—a wonderful, golden city that exists only in the imagination. In 2006, Ali Ould Sidi traveled from Timbuktu to England on a cultural mission. "It is sad to discover," he said to some new English friends, "that most people in your country do not think we are real."

❻ There's an airport in Timbuktu now, so traveling there is a lot easier than it used to be. If flying in seems too easy, you can take a boat up the Niger River,[18] or try to make it overland.[19] However you go, don't  expect the real Timbuktu to be like the imaginary one. If you know what you're looking at, Timbuktu is a fascinating[20] place. It's also flat, dusty and hot. The buildings are mostly made of mud—not gold. And you're probably going to get sand in your eyes—*real* sand.

Ⓦ Ⓞ Ⓡ Ⓓ Ⓛ Ⓘ Ⓢ Ⓣ

18. Niger River〔ˋnaɪdʒɚ ˏrɪvɚ〕 *n.* 尼日河
19. overland〔ˋovɚˏlænd〕 *adv.* 經由陸路
20. fascinating〔ˋfæsn̩ˏetɪŋ〕 *adj.* 迷人的；很有趣的

譯文

❶ 廷巴克圖：它是真的嗎？抑或它是虛構的地方，就像亞馬遜叢林的埃爾多拉多，或是海底的亞特蘭提斯島？其實它兩者都是。

❷ 廷巴克圖是個真實的地方。它是馬利的城鎮，位在撒哈拉沙漠的西南邊緣，大約有 3 萬人居住在那裡。對非洲人來說，有好幾百年，廷巴克圖都是重要的區域貿易中心。來自北方的商隊從沙漠把鹽帶來，並帶著黃金與奴隸回去。

❸ 思想也跟著商隊旅行，所以時間一久，廷巴克圖就成了穆斯林學者的重要中心。廷巴克圖有三座著名的清真寺，最古老的金蓋雷貝爾清真寺建於 1327 年，桑科雷清真寺和西迪葉海亞清真寺也有數百年之久。14 世紀時，桑科雷大學擁有全世界其中一座最大的圖書館，可容納 2 萬 5,000 個學生。他們研讀可蘭經的伊斯蘭教義，以及數學、地理、歷史、物理、天文學和化學之類的學科。對非洲人來說，廷巴克圖現在和過去都是生活、讀書和做生意的地方。它是個存在地圖上的地方。

❹ 對歐洲人來說，廷巴克圖向來是個地圖上「沒有」的地方、傳說中的城市、撒哈拉的珍珠、非洲的埃爾多拉多。1824 年時，巴黎的法國地理學會懸賞 1 萬法郎給第一個前往廷巴克圖而能活著回來的非穆斯林人。來自蘇格蘭的戈登．萊恩在 1826 年成功抵達，卻被一些當地居民殺害。兩年後，法國人勒內．卡耶拿到了獎賞。他偽裝成穆斯林，獨自往返了廷巴克圖。

❺ 在歐洲，廷巴克圖這幾個字長久以來都被當成一種比喻。當大家說到「廷巴克圖」時，他們指的是一個有異國情調且不易前往的遙遠地方。很多歐美人士仍然相信廷巴克圖是個傳說，這個了不起的黃金城只存在於想像中。

2006 年時，阿里・奧德・西迪率領文化代表團從廷巴克圖來到英國。他對一些英國的新朋友說：「令人感傷的發現是，貴國大部分的民眾並不認為我們是真的。」

6 廷巴克圖現在有個機場，所以去那裡要比以往容易許多。假如搭飛機看起來太過輕鬆，那你可以坐船上溯尼日河，或是設法由陸路前往。不管你怎麼去，可別以為真正的廷巴克圖就跟想像中一樣。假如你知道自己在看的是什麼，廷巴克圖會是個迷人的地方。它同時也很平坦、多塵與炎熱。建築多半是用泥土所建造──而不是黃金。而且你的眼睛八成會進沙，而且是「真正的」沙。

🔑 精要句型

■ **Gordon Laing from Scotland made it there in 1826, *only to* get killed by some locals.**

來自蘇格蘭的戈登・萊恩在 1826 年成功抵達，卻被一些當地居民殺害。

句型 **..., only to ...** 「……，但卻……」

在本句中，「only to」是在導入第二件多半令人遺憾的事，並跟句子中第一部分所發生的事有關。

例句 Nick was accepted into medical school, *only to* discover he couldn't afford the tuition.

尼克錄取了醫院學，但卻發現自己付不起學費。

After a long, hard day, Gina finally arrived home, *only to* discover that her house had burned down.

經過漫長而辛苦的一天，吉娜終於回到家，但卻發現她的房子被燒光了。

✏️ 詞彙測驗

( ) **1.** Which of the following definitions of **real** describes how the word is used in paragraph 5, line 7?

A. not imaginary but existing in fact

B. Brazilian money

C. important or special in some way

D. genuine, not fake or artificial

( ) **2.** Which of the following definitions of **back** describes how the word is used in paragraph 4, line 7?

A. to give support or approval

B. the part of a person or thing opposite from the front

C. to return to an original place or condition

D. the part of a chair that you lean against when you sit

(　　) **3.** Which of the following definitions of **center** describes how the word is used in paragraph 3, line 3?

A. the middle of an object or an area

B. to focus upon something

C. a place important for some activity

D. to move something to the middle of a space

 旅 遊 一 點 通

想要溯河去廷巴克圖嗎？那你就得在泥屋村中過夜。馬利住了各式各樣的部落：班巴拉人、多貢人和圖阿格雷人等等。有時村民很友善，有時則不然。河馬和鱷魚則通常一點也不友善。琪拉‧賽拉克（Kira Salak）有本書叫做《最殘酷的旅程》（*The Cruelest Journey: Six Hundred Miles to Timbuktu*），把裡面有關尼日河之旅的部分全部看一遍吧：

http://www.kirasalak.com/Cruelest.html

旅遊好用句
廷巴克圖沒有太多的禮品店，但可以找到手工籃子、陶器和木雕。只要問一下：

Do you know where I can buy some local handicrafts?
「你知道我可以去哪裡買一些本地的手工藝品嗎？」

解答

詞彙測驗

1. 在「real」的下列定義中，哪一個是在描述這個字在第五段第七行中的用法？

A. 不是憑空想像，而是實際存在

B. 巴西貨幣

C. 在某方面重要或特別

D. 真品，不是冒牌或人造的

Ans A

2. 在「back」的下列定義中，哪一個是在描述這個字在第四段第七行中的用法？

A. 支持或贊成

B. 人或物與正面相反的部位

C. 回到原本的地方或狀態

D. 就座時椅子上可以靠的部分

Ans C

3. 在「center」的下列定義中，哪一個是在描述這個字在第三段第三行中的用法？

A. 物件或地區的中間

B. 專注在某事上

C. 某項活動的重要地方

D. 把東西移到中間地帶

Ans C

PART 2

亞洲和大洋洲

UNIT 4

Kiyomizu-dera
清水寺

Located in Japan（日本）

❶ On a hill overlooking[1] Kyoto,[2] surrounded by cherry trees, is Kiyomizu-dera, a Buddhist temple the Japanese consider a national treasure. People love to visit Kiyomizu-dera not just to appreciate the natural and spiritual beauty of the place, but also because they can drink magic water, consider a wish-fulfilling leap[3] from the high terrace,[4] and try walking with closed eyes from one love stone to the other.

❷ Kiyomizu-dera means "Pure Water Temple." The place takes its name from the clear waterfall that flows down a hill to the temple, where it is directed into three streams. People who drink the sacred[5] water are said to be blessed

with health, long life and wisdom. Long-handled cups are available for visitors. The only catch[6] is that drinking from *all* three streams is considered greedy—it brings bad luck. So you have to make a choice. Wisdom seems like a no-brainer[7] first drink. Perhaps it will make your next choice a little easier. On the other hand, if you believe that ignorance[8] is bliss, maybe you'll prefer to skip wisdom and try for a long,

Ⓦⓞⓡⓓ Ⓛⓘⓢⓣ

1. overlook〔͵ovɚˋlʊk〕*v.* 俯視；俯瞰
2. Kyoto〔ˋkjoto〕*n.* 京都市（位於日本本州南部）
3. leap〔lip〕*n.* 跳躍
4. terrace〔ˋtɛrɪs〕*n.* 梯台；梯形地的一層
5. sacred〔ˋsekrɪd〕*adj.* 神聖的
6. catch〔kætʃ〕*n.*【口語】陷阱；圈套
7. no-brainer〔ˋno ͵brenɚ〕*adj.*【俚】不需要動腦都可做的；很容易的

healthy life. It's up to you.

❸ The temple standing today was constructed in 1633 upon the same site where the original temple was built eight centuries earlier. Supported by 139 wooden pillars[9] (not a single nail was used!), a large open-air[10] deck[11] extends from the main hall of the temple out over the hillside.[12] From there, you can see the whole city of Kyoto spread out in the valley below. During Japan's Edo period (1603-1868), 234 people are known to have leaped from this stage, believing that if they survived, they would be granted a wish. The platform[13] is 13 meters high, so it was about like jumping from a fourth-story window. Most of the leapers survived. About fifteen percent did not.

❹ These days, leaping from the terrace is not encouraged. If for some reason you are determined to try it, take a short timeout[14] and have a

8. ignorance〔ˋɪgnərəns〕 *n.* 無知
9. pillar〔ˋpɪlə〕 *n.* 柱
10. open-air〔ˋopənˋɛr〕 *adj.* 露天的；戶外的
11. deck〔dɛk〕 *n.* 地板
12. hillside〔ˋhɪlˏsaɪd〕 *n.* 山腰；山坡
13. platform〔ˋplætˏfɔrm〕 *n.* 台；講台
14. timeout〔ˋtaɪmˋaut〕 *n.* 暫停

sip[15] of wisdom water. Think it through. You do have options. You could, for example, just buy a postcard and call it a day.[16] If leaping still seems like the best plan, pause one last time so that you can take a big drink from the stream of long life.

❺ Next—assuming you're still able to walk—it'll be time to visit the love stones. There are two of them, set in the ground 18 meters apart in a shrine[17] dedicated[18] to Okuninushi, god of love and perfect matches. Close your eyes and try to walk from one stone to the other. If you make it, it means you will soon find true love. If you miss—well, what does a stupid stone know anyway?

ⓌⓄⓇⒹ ⓁⒾⓈⓉ

15. sip〔sɪp〕 *n.* 一啜；一口
16. call it a day 到此為止
17. shrine〔ʃraɪn〕 *n.* 廟；祠
18. dedicate〔`dɛdəˌket〕 *v.* 奉獻；獻給

50

譯文

❶ 清水寺位在一座可俯瞰京都市的山丘上，四周都是櫻花樹，是被日本人視為國寶的一間佛寺。民眾愛去清水寺不僅是為了欣賞當地的天然與心靈美景，也是因為能喝到神水，能考慮從高處梯台往下跳以實現願望，還能試著閉上眼睛從其中一顆戀愛石走到另一顆。

❷ Kiyomizu-dera 的意思是「清水寺」。得名自從山丘上流到寺廟的清澈瀑布，瀑布在此處流入三道水泉。據說喝過此聖水的人可保佑健康、長壽與智慧。遊客有長柄杓可以取用。唯一的陷阱是，把三道水泉的水「都」喝了，會被視為貪心而招致惡運。所以你必須做個選擇。智慧似乎是理所當然的第一選擇，也許它會讓你的下一個選擇容易一些。反過來說，如果你覺得無知是種福氣，也許你寧可跳過智慧，而去祈求健康與長壽。決定權在你。

❸ 現今屹立的寺廟興建於 1633 年，和早了八世紀所建立的原本寺廟位於同一個地方。由 139 根木頭柱子支撐（一根釘子都沒用上！），一大片露天地板從寺廟的正殿往外延伸到山坡上。從那個地方，你可以看到整個京都城在底下的山谷綿延開來。在日本的江戶時代（1603 到 1868 年），據載有 234 人從這個高台往下跳，他們相信如果能活下來，他們就能實現一個願望。這個高台有 13 公尺高，所以這就像是從四樓的窗戶往下跳。跳的人大部分都活了下來，約有一成五的人沒能成功。

❹ 如今並不鼓勵從高台往下跳。如果你基於某種原因而決心一試，請稍微暫停一下，喝一口智慧水泉，好好想一想吧。你是有其他選擇的。比方說，你可以乾脆買張明信片，並就此打住。如果往下跳仍然是你的最好計畫，那再暫停最後一次，去喝一大杯長壽水泉的水吧。

❺ 接下來——假設你還能走路的話——就是參觀戀愛石的時間了。神殿的地上擺了相隔 18 公尺的兩顆，殿內則供奉了大國主，也就是撮合良緣的愛神。閉上你的眼睛，試著從其中一顆石頭走向另一顆。假如你成功走到了，這代表你很快就能找到真愛。假如你沒成功，呃，反正一顆笨石頭懂什麼呢？

🔑 精要句型

■ **People love to visit Kiyomizu-dera *not just* to appreciate the natural beauty of the place, *but also* because they can drink magic water.**
民眾愛去清水寺「不僅是」為了欣賞當地的天然美景，「也是」因為能喝到神水。

句型 **X not just Y, but also Z.**「X 不僅是 Y，也是 Z。」
X 有兩個原因：Y 和 Z。

例句 Joy decided not to go to Harvard, *not just* because it cost too much, *but also* because she was not accepted for admission.
喬依決定不去念哈佛，「不僅是」因為它太花錢了，「也是」因為她沒有被錄取。

Patrick likes Taichung better than Taipei *not just* for the sunshine, *but also* because it is cheaper to live there.
派屈克比較喜歡台中而不是台北，「不僅是」因為有陽光，「也是」因為在那裡過日子比較便宜。

 詞彙測驗

一、**Translate each Chinese phrase by using words and phrases from the essay.**

　　a) 你是有所選擇的。　＿＿＿＿＿＿＿＿＿＿＿＿＿＿

　　b) 稍微暫停一下　＿＿＿＿＿＿＿＿＿＿＿＿＿＿

　　c) 它招致惡運　＿＿＿＿＿＿＿＿＿＿＿＿＿＿

　　d) 往下跳並不被鼓勵　＿＿＿＿＿＿＿＿＿＿＿＿＿＿

　　e) 心靈美景　＿＿＿＿＿＿＿＿＿＿＿＿＿＿

　　f) 無知是種福氣　＿＿＿＿＿＿＿＿＿＿＿＿＿＿

二、**Which sentence in each pair is true?**

_____ A "no-brainer" decision makes you feel dumb, like you have no brain.

_____ A "no-brainer" decision is so easy to make, you don't have to use your brain.

_____ Bliss feels really good.

_____ Bliss feels really bad.

_____ You can often find shrines within temples.

_____ You can often find temples within shrines.

旅 遊 一 點 通

清水寺本身很好玩，「前往」清水寺也很好玩。從京都站（該站很酷的未來感設計跟傳統寺廟形成強烈的對比）搭公車（100 號或 206 號）或計程車到東山區（Higashiyama district），並跟著人群往山上的寺廟走。當地的街道既狹窄又有趣，成排的商店裡滿是伴手禮和當地的特產。假如你在四月初前往，可以看到櫻花盛開。看看下列網站，以徹底了解京都的公車要怎麼搭：

http://www.city.kyoto.jp/koho/eng/access/transport.html

旅遊好用句

假如你決定搭計程車，那就要確定自己搭得起：

Excuse me. About how much will it cost to go to Kiyomizu-dera?

「請問一下，去清水寺大概要多少錢？」

解 答

 詞彙測驗

一、利用文章中的單字及片語來翻譯下列中文。

a) You do have options.

b) take a short timeout

c) it brings bad luck

d) leaping is not encouraged

e) spiritual beauty

f) ignorance is bliss

二、各組句子中的哪句話是正確的？

＿＿ 「想都不必想」的決定使你感覺起來很蠢，彷彿你沒有腦子一樣。

T 「想都不必想」的決定是輕而易舉，使你不必花腦筋。

T 福氣感覺起來好極了。

＿＿ 福氣感覺起來糟透了。

T 你經常可以在寺廟裡找到神殿。

＿＿ 你經常可以在神殿裡找到寺廟。

Angkor Wat
吳哥窟

Located in Cambodia（柬埔寨）

❶ You've seen the lists: one thousand—or fifty—or twenty-eight—places to see before you die. What if you had to make a list of just one? If you ask experienced travelers for advice, one place comes up again and again: Angkor Wat, City of Temples, pride of Cambodia.[1]

❷ Angkor Wat is a beautiful, spiritually inspiring,[2] really old, exotic,[3] cool, fascinating,[4] one-of-a-kind[5] place. Hindus[6] love it. Buddhists love it. Lara Croft, of *Tomb Raider* fame, had her best adventures there. Two million tourists visit every year and few leave disappointed. After his visit, Italian writer Tiziano Terzani said that Angkor Wat was one of the few places in the world that made him proud to be a member of the human race.

❸ From the 9th century to the 15th, Angkor was the capital of the Khmer[7] Empire. As many as one million people lived in the city, which sprawled[8] over an area of 1,000 square kilometers (modern London covers about 700 square kilometers). There were many temples in the city. The most famous and well preserved[9] of them, Angkor Wat, was built by King Saryavaram II in the 12th century.

Ⓦ Ⓞ Ⓡ Ⓓ Ⓛ Ⓘ Ⓢ Ⓣ

1. Cambodia 〔kæm`bodɪə〕 *n.* 柬埔寨（中南半島南部的一國）
2. inspiring 〔ɪn`spaɪrɪŋ〕 *adj.* 啓發靈感的；鼓舞的
3. exotic 〔ɪg`zɑtɪk〕 *adj.* 異國情調的
4. fascinating 〔`fæsn̩ˌetɪŋ〕 *adj.* 迷人的；很有趣的
5. one-of-a-kind 獨一無二的
6. Hindu 〔`hɪndu〕 *n.* 印度教徒
7. Khmer 〔kmɛr〕 *n.* 高棉族人
8. sprawl 〔sprɔl〕 *v.* 紊亂地散開；蔓延
9. preserve 〔prɪ`zɝv〕 *v.* 保存

❹ Angkor Wat is big. It may be the largest religious structure ever built. Khmer architects used as much stone to build Angkor Wat as the ancient Egyptians[10] did for the Pyramid of Cheops. Angkor Wat was

originally dedicated[11] to the Hindu god Lord Vishnu (he's the one with four arms and lotus[12] eyes). The five perfectly symmetrical[13] towers of the temple symbolize[14] the five peaks[15] of Vishnu's home, Mount Meru.

❺ Many of the stones used in the building are carved into intricate[16] figures and mysterious smiling faces. Pictures on stone walls show scenes from the great holy books of Hinduism,[17] the Ramayana and Mahabharata. Inscriptions[18] in

10. Egyptian〔ɪˋdʒɪpʃən〕*n.* 埃及人　*adj.* 埃及（人）的
11. dedicate〔ˋdɛdə͵ket〕*v.* 奉獻
12. lotus〔ˋlotəs〕*n.* 睡蓮
13. symmetrical〔sɪˋmɛtrɪkl̩〕*adj.* 左右對稱的；相稱的
14. symbolize〔ˋsɪmbl͵aɪz〕*v.* 象徵
15. peak〔pik〕*n.* 尖端；頂點
16. intricate〔ˋɪntrəkɪt〕*adj.* 錯綜的；複雜的
17. Hinduism〔ˋhɪndu͵ɪzəm〕*n.* 印度教
18. inscription〔ɪnˋskrɪpʃən〕*n.* 刻；碑文

Sanskrit[19] and Khmer tell of great battles won by Khmer kings and heroes. The temple is like a giant library of poems, stories and history, all written in stone.

❻ You don't need to understand all that to appreciate Angkor Wat. No matter what language you speak or where you come from, the place works its magic on you. Many visitors are particularly moved by the beautiful way the temples are aging and decaying.[20] In some places, the roots of giant trees are wrapped[21] like witches' fingers around walls and fallen stones. If you ask around, you can

find one tree that looks just like a human butt. That's probably not what made Mr. Terzani feel proud to be human, but, according to the locals,[22] rubbing[23] the butt does bring good luck. Is it true? There's only one way to find out. Go. Once you make it to Angkor Wat, you can already count yourself lucky.

Ⓦ Ⓞ Ⓡ Ⓓ Ⓛ Ⓘ Ⓢ Ⓣ

19. Sanskrit〔ˋsænskrɪt〕 *n.* 梵文
20. decay〔dɪˋke〕 *v.* 腐敗；腐爛
21. wrap〔ræp〕 *v.* 包；裹
22. local〔ˋlokļ〕 *n.* 當地居民
23. rub〔rʌb〕 *v.* 摩擦；搓；揉

譯文

❶ 你已經看過這樣的清單：在你死前要去參觀的 1,000 個、50 個或 28 個地方。萬一你要列的清單只限一個地方呢？如果你請旅遊老手們提供建議，有個地方會一而再地出現：吳哥窟——寺廟之城，柬埔寨之光。

❷ 吳哥窟是個美麗、啓發心靈、十分古老、有異國情調、很酷、迷人、獨一無二的地方。印度人愛它，佛教徒愛它，因《古墓奇兵》而聞名的羅拉·卡芙特在那裡經歷了她最棒的冒險（註：《古墓奇兵》曾在吳哥窟取景拍攝）。每年有 200 萬個遊客到此參觀，鮮少有人失望而歸。義大利作家帝奇亞諾·坦尚尼參觀之後說，世界上有少數的地方會令他以身為人類的一員感到光榮，而吳哥窟就是其中之一。

❸ 從第 9 世紀到 15 世紀，吳哥是高棉帝國的首都。該城住了多達 100 萬人，占地達 1,000 平方公里（現代倫敦的面積大約是 700 平方公里）。城內有許多寺廟，其中最負盛名與保存最好的就是吳哥窟，它是在 12 世紀時由蘇耶跋摩二世國王所興建。

❹ 吳哥窟很大，可能是歷來所興建最大的宗教結構體。高棉的建築師在蓋吳哥窟時，所用的石頭跟古埃及人在蓋基奧普斯金字塔時一樣多。吳哥窟原本是在供奉印度教的神祇毗濕奴神（祂有四條手臂與蓮花眼）。五座完全對稱的寺塔則是象徵毗濕奴居住地須彌山的五座山峰。

❺ 建築所用的石頭，很多都被雕刻成精細複雜的人物形象和神秘笑臉。石牆上的圖案所呈現的景象，是取自印度教的偉大聖經《羅摩耶那》和《摩訶波羅多》。梵文和高棉文的銘刻訴說著高棉的國王和英雄所打的大勝仗。這座廟有如巨大的博物館，收藏了詩歌、故事和歷史，而且全都寫在石頭上。

❻ 你不必了解這一切，也能好好欣賞吳哥窟。無論你說的是哪種語言、從哪裡來，這個地方都會對你施展魔法。寺廟以其美妙的方式老朽著，尤其讓許多遊客動容。在某些地方，巨木的根纏繞在牆壁與落石的四周，宛如女巫的手指。如果你四處打聽，你會發現有一棵樹看起來就像人的屁股。坦尚尼大概不是因為它，才以身為人類為榮。但據當地民眾表示，摸摸這個屁股的確會帶來好運。是真的嗎？只有一個方法能搞清楚。出發吧！等你抵達吳哥窟，你就已經可以說自己走運了。

精要句型

■ *Lara Croft, of Tomb Raider fame*, had her best adventures there.
因《古墓奇兵》而聞名的蘿拉‧卡芙特，在那裡經歷了她最棒的冒險。

句型 **Person, of X fame, ...** 「因 X 而聞名的某人，……。」
此句型可以幫助讀者回想這個人到底是誰。

例句 *Bill Gates, of Microsoft fame*, has given millions of dollars to charity.
因微軟而聞名的比爾‧蓋茲，捐了數百萬美元的善款。

The lovely Kristen Stewart, of Twilight fame, was even more beautiful in *Adventureland*.
因《暮光之城》而聞名的美女克莉絲汀‧史都華，在《畢業即失業》裡更美。

詞彙測驗

一、In paragraph 5, line 2, the writer uses the phrase "intricate figures." Intricate means "having many complexly arranged elements; elaborate" (*American Heritage Dictionary*). For each of the following pairs, choose the word that is most likely to appear after intricate.

1. _____ intricate carvings
   _____ intricate roads

2. _____ intricate buildings
   _____ intricate details

3. _____ intricate word
   _____ intricate design

4. _____ intricate system

_____ intricate advice

5. _____ intricate tests

_____ intricate patterns

二、**Look in the essay to find antonyms of these words.**

1. familiar _____

2. tourists _____

3. unbalanced _____

4. simple _____

5. unholy _____

旅 遊 一 點 通

遊客都不喜歡下雨。在 11 月到 4 月的乾季期間，造訪吳哥窟的人最多。
不過，在 7 月這個雨季的降雨高峰，柬埔寨卻是一片翠綠、美不勝收。
雲層和夕陽相當壯觀，每天通常只會下一、兩個小時的大雨，旅館房間
也最便宜。如果你不介意弄得有點濕，那就在雨季前往吳哥窟吧。

想對參觀吳哥窟有更多的了解，可以參閱下列網站：

http://www.timesonline.co.uk/tol/travel/your_say/article642995.ece

旅遊好用句
如果突然碰上大雨，可以詢問周遭民眾：

Excuse me, where can I buy an umbrella around here?
「不好意思，請問附近哪裡可以買到傘？」

解答

詞彙測驗

一、在第五段的第二行中，作者用了「intricate figures」這個說法。Intricate 意指「有許多經過複雜安排的元素；精心的」（《美國傳統字典》）。從下列各組搭配詞中，分別選出比較可能出現在 intricate 後面的字。

1. intricate carvings 精密的雕刻

2. intricate details 精密的細節

3. intricate design 精密的設計

4. intricate system 精密的系統

5. intricate patterns 精密的樣式

二、從文中找出這些單字的反義字。

1. exotic 外來的；有異國情調的

2. locals 當地人

3. symmetrical 對稱的

4. intricate 精細的

5. holy 神聖的

UNIT 6 | The Great Wall of China 中國長城

Located in China（中國）

❶ To appreciate the importance of the Great Wall of China, imagine that you are a farmer living north of Beijing, early in the 13ᵗʰ century. You're working outside. It's a nice sunny day. Suddenly the ground begins to tremble and you hear a terrifying noise: galloping[1] warhorses.[2] Mongols.[3] There is no time to run or hide. They can shoot arrows while they ride. The arrows do not miss. They are upon you, they are ferocious[4] and their policy is simple: surrender, or die.

❷ The Great Wall was a serious obstacle[5] for men on horseback. It forced them to slow down and look for gaps. This gave the men defending the wall extra time to organize. Smoke and fire signals were used to communicate warnings and calls

for help from one watchtower[6] to the next, all the way along the wall. New soldiers could arrive quickly by using the top of the wall as a road through rough country.

Ⓦⓞⓡⓓ Ⓛⓘⓢⓣ

1. gallop〔ˋɡæləp〕 v. 疾馳；飛奔
2. warhorse〔ˋwɔrˏhɔrs〕 n. 戰馬
3. Mongol〔ˋmɑŋɡəl〕 n. 蒙古人
4. ferocious〔fəˋroʃəs〕 adj. 兇猛的；殘暴的
5. obstacle〔ˋɑbstəkl〕 n. 障礙（物）
6. watchtower〔ˋwɑtʃˏtauɚ〕 n. 守望樓；瞭望台

❸ The Great Wall was not built all at once. Some sections were built as early as the 5th century BC. Construction continued off and on until modern times. The main idea was always to keep Mongols (and other nomads)[7] out. In the 3rd century BC, the Great Wall also played a part as various warring[8] Chinese kingdoms were united under the Qin Dynasty. The Wall protected the Qin state, and held it together.

❹ In the 13th century, the Mongols were too strong. No wall could stop them. Kublai Khan's armies conquered[9] all of China. The Yuan Dynasty was a Mongol Dynasty. During that period, the Great Wall was just a wall. The Mongols did not need it for protection. Their empire stretched all the way to Europe.

❺ Towards the end of the 14th century, the Chinese drove the Mongols back north. To encourage them to stay there, the Ming Dynasty extended the Great Wall all the way across northern China, from Hebei province[10] in the east to Gansu province in the west. Including the gaps where rivers and mountains offer good natural defense, the Wall is more than 8,850 kilometers long. Building it was a tremendous[11] feat[12] of engineering and political organization.

7. nomad 〔`nomæd〕 *n.* 遊牧部落的人
8. warring 〔`wɔrɪŋ〕 *adj.* 交戰中的；敵對的
9. conquer 〔`kɑŋkə〕 *v.* 征服
10. province 〔`prɑvɪns〕 *n.* 省
11. tremendous 〔trɪ`mɛndəs〕 *adj.* 巨大的；驚人的
12. feat 〔fit〕 *n.* 功績；功勞

6 The Great Wall helped keep the Ming relatively safe for almost three centuries. Then, in 1644, China was again conquered from the north, by the Manchus.[13] How did the Manchus get past the wall? The story involves a  Ming general, a beautiful woman named Yuenyuen, and a rebel[14] Chinese warlord[15] who temporarily seized control of Beijing. The Great Wall could not protect China from trouble that came from within. End result: the Wall was left defenseless[16] and the Manchu army walked right through the gates.

W O R D L I S T

13. Manchu 〔mæn`tʃu〕 *n.* 滿族人
14. rebel 〔`rɛbl〕 *adj.* 叛逆的；背叛的
15. warlord 〔`wɔr͵lɔrd〕 *n.* 軍閥
16. defenseless 〔dɪ`fɛnslɪs〕 *adj.* 無防備的；不設防的

譯文

❶ 為了體認中國長城的重要性，想像一下你是 13 世紀初住在北京北方的農人。你正在戶外工作，天氣很好，陽光普照。突然地面開始顫動，你聽到了可怕的聲響：奔馳的戰馬。蒙古人。要逃或躲都來不及了。他們能一邊騎馬一邊射箭，而且百發百中。他們追上你了；他們很凶殘；而且他們的規則很簡單：不投降，就得死。

❷ 對馬背上的人而言，長城是個艱困的障礙。迫使他們放慢速度、尋找缺口。如此一來，守牆的人就有多餘的時間可以組織起來。狼煙和烽火信號被用來示警與呼救，一路沿著長城的瞭望台一個接一個傳下去。把長城頂端當作道路來穿越難走的地區，新增的兵援就能迅速抵達。

❸ 長城並不是一次就建造完成，有些段落早在西元前五世紀就已建造。建築工程一直斷斷續續，直到近代為止。它的主要構想一直都是要把蒙古人（和其他遊牧民族）阻擋在外。在西元前三世紀，當各個交戰的諸侯國在秦朝被統一時，長城也扮演了要角。長城保護了秦國，使它凝聚在一起。

❹ 到了 13 世紀，蒙古人太強大了，沒有一座牆擋得住他們。忽必烈的軍隊征服了整個中國，元朝就是蒙古人的朝代。在那段期間，長城只是座牆而已，蒙古人不需要它來保護。他們的帝國一路擴展到了歐洲。

❺ 在 14 世紀接近尾聲時，漢人把蒙古人趕回了北方。為了促使他們留在那裡，明朝在中國北方擴建長城，一路從東邊的河北省，橫跨至西邊的甘肅省。包括有河流與山脈提供良好天然屏障的隘口在內，長城超過 8,850 公里長。建造它在工程與政治的組織動員上都是了不起的功績。

❻ 有將近三個世紀，長城把明朝保護得相當安全。後來到了 1644 年，中國再次被來自北方的滿人所征服。滿人是如何通關進入長城的呢？這個故事牽涉到一位明朝將軍、一位名叫陳圓圓的美麗女子，以及一個叛變造反並暫時掌控北京的漢人軍閥。長城無法保護中國免於內亂，最後的結局就是，長城毫無防禦，滿人的軍隊長驅直入。

🔑 精要句型

■ **New soldiers could arrive quickly *by using* the top of the wall as a road through rough country.**

把長城頂端當作道路來穿越難走的地區，新增的兵援就能迅速抵達。

句型 **do X by Y-ing**「藉由做 Y，就能 X」

這個句型用來描述做 Y 這件事，以達到 X 的效果。

例句 Believe it or not, Hanna lost 12 kg *by eating* nothing but bacon for six weeks.

信不信由你，靠著只吃培根六個星期，漢娜減了 12 公斤。

I'm going to convince her to forgive me *by cooking* her favorite dish: Guangdong noodles.

靠著做她最愛吃的菜——廣式麵條，我要說服她原諒我。

✏️ 詞彙測驗

一、**Which sentence in each pair is true?**

_____ An obstacle slows you down.

_____ An obstacle speeds you up.

_____ A nomad is a special kind of Chinese soldier.

_____ A nomad is a person with no permanent home.

_____ The Mongols were famous for conquering.

_____ The Mongols were famous for surrendering.

二、**Use words and phrases from the essay to translate each item from Chinese.**

    a) 全部同時地　＿＿＿＿＿＿＿＿＿＿＿

    b) 斷斷續續地　＿＿＿＿＿＿＿＿＿＿＿

    c) 扮演其中一角；在某方面起作用　＿＿＿＿＿＿＿＿＿＿＿

    d) 在秦朝時被統一　＿＿＿＿＿＿＿＿＿＿＿

    e) 無防禦力的　＿＿＿＿＿＿＿＿＿＿＿

    f) 最後的結局　＿＿＿＿＿＿＿＿＿＿＿

 旅 遊 一 點 通

大部分的人都是以一日遊的方式從北京去參觀長城。假如你想要有一車車的遊客作伴，住處就要靠近北京。長城的八達嶺部分最受觀光團歡迎，慕天峪和黃驊等段則距離比較遠，比較不擠。如果你的腳力不錯，不妨考慮沿著金山嶺和司馬台之間的長城走上 7.5 公里。看看下列網頁的資料，裡面介紹了從北京可以到達的各段長城：

http://gochina.about.com/od/whattoseeinbeijing/p/BJ_VisitGW.htm

旅遊好用句

八達嶺四周賣紀念品的攤販是出了名地會死纏爛打。假如他們跟在你身邊想要賣東西給你，你可以假裝不會說中文：

Please, don't waste your time talking with me. I won't buy anything.
「拜託，不用浪費時間跟我說了。我什麼都不會買的。」

詞彙測驗

一、各組句子中的哪句話是正確的？

_T_ 阻礙會讓你減速。
___ 阻礙會讓你加速。

___ 遊牧民族是特殊的中國兵種。
_T_ 遊牧民族是沒有永久住所的人。

_T_ 蒙古人以征戰而聞名。
___ 蒙古人以投降而聞名。

二、利用文章中的單字及片語來翻譯下列中文。

a) all at once

b) off and on

c) play a part

d) be united under the Qin Dynasty

e) be left defenseless

f) end result

UNIT 7 | **Red Square**
紅場

Located in Russia（俄羅斯）

❶ Moscow's famous Red Square is actually a rectangle,[1] 400 meters long and 150 meters wide. It is an open space in the center of the city, surrounded by some of the most important buildings in Russia. A tour around the Red Square works as a crash[2] course in Russia's history of Tsars,[3] saints[4] and Soviets.[5]

❷ Saint Basil's Cathedral,[6] located at the south end of the Red Square, is the building people think of when they think of Russia. The church's fantastically[7] colorful, onion-shaped domes[8] are meant to represent the flames of a giant fire, rising into the sky. The cathedral was built in the 16th century by the Tsar (King) Ivan the Terrible. It was a monument[9] to a military victory in which Ivan's forces had defeated and massacred[10] the population of a city called Kazan.

❸ Later, the church became associated with Saint Basil, who is buried there. Basil was a shoemaker who never wore shoes. Even during the

---

Ⓦ Ⓞ Ⓡ Ⓓ Ⓛ Ⓘ Ⓢ Ⓣ

1. **rectangle** 〔ˋrɛktæŋgl〕 *n.* 長方形
2. **crash** 〔kræʃ〕 *adj.* 速成的；一氣呵成的
3. **tsar** 〔tsɑr〕 *n.* 舊時俄國的皇帝；沙皇
4. **saint** 〔sent〕 *n.* 聖徒；聖人
5. **Soviet** 〔ˋsovɪɪt〕 *n.* 蘇聯政府；蘇聯國民
6. **cathedral** 〔kəˋθidrəl〕 *n.* 大教堂
7. **fantastically** 〔fænˋtæstɪk]ɪ〕 *adv.* 【口語】極好地；很棒地

freezing Russian winter, he went about barefoot.[11] For Basil, clothing was also optional. To make a political point sometimes he wore nothing but chains. Surviving winter without clothes was one of Basil's miracles. He hung around markets and taverns,[12] teaching kindness, and he was one of the very few people in Russia who dared to criticize Ivan the Terrible.

❹ Just a few steps from Saint Basil's, on the west side of Red Square, is the Kremlin.[13] In Russian, kremlin means fortress,[14] or castle. Many Russian towns have kremlins. The Kremlin on the Red Square has been the center of Russian political power for hundreds of years. Ivan the Terrible, Catherine the Great, Lenin and Stalin all did memorable[15] work at the Kremlin.

❺ Right outside the Kremlin, towards the north end of the Red Square, is Lenin's Tomb. There's only one place to go if you want to see Lenin's

8. dome〔dom〕*n.* 圓屋頂
9. monument〔`mɑnjəmənt〕*n.* 紀念碑
10. massacre〔`mæsəkɚ〕*v.* 屠殺
11. barefoot〔`bɛrˌfut〕*adv.* 赤腳地
12. tavern〔`tævən〕*n.* 酒店；酒館
13. Kremlin〔`krɛmlɪn〕*n.* 克里姆林宮
14. fortress〔`fɔrtrɪs〕*n.* 要塞；堅固的場所
15. memorable〔`mɛmərəbl〕*adj.* 值得紀念的；難忘的

dead body, and this is it. Vladimir Lenin was a workaholic[16] revolutionary[17] who became the first leader of the Soviet Union. His body has been on public display since he died in 1924. A special organization, the Research Institute for Biological Structures, is in charge of keeping him looking good.

6 The lines at Lenin's Tomb aren't as long as they used to be. Lots of people walk right on by on their way to the State Historical Museum, just north of the Kremlin, or, more often, to Russia's most famous mall, GUM, which makes up the entire eastern side of the Red Square. GUM (say "goom") stands for *Glavnyi Universalnyi Magazin*—"State Department Store." Think Burberry, Puma and Calvin Klein. Saint Basil probably wouldn't have been much interested, but nowadays few Red Square visitors are able to resist a bit of shopping at GUM.

16. workaholic〔͵wɜkə`hɑlɪk〕*n.* 工作狂
17. revolutionary〔͵rɛvə`luʃən͵ɛrɪ〕*n.* 革命者

譯文

❶ 莫斯科著名的紅場其實是長方形，長 400 公尺，寬 150 公尺。它是個位於市中心的開放空間，四周有一些俄羅斯最重要的建築。繞著紅場一遊，等於上了一堂沙皇、聖人與蘇聯等俄羅斯歷史的速成課。

❷ 聖巴索大教堂位於紅場的南端。大家一想到俄羅斯，就會想到這座建築。教堂五彩繽紛的洋蔥形圓頂是用來表現巨大火光的火焰直衝天際。這座大教堂是由沙皇（國王）恐怖伊凡在 16 世紀所興建，以紀念一場軍事勝利：伊凡的軍隊擊敗並屠殺了喀山這個城市的居民。

❸ 後來該教堂變得跟聖巴索有關，他葬於此地。巴索是個鞋匠，但從來不穿鞋。即使在嚴寒的俄羅斯冬天，他還是赤著腳到處走。對巴索來說，衣服也是可有可無。為了陳述政治論點，有時候他什麼都不穿，只戴著枷鎖。不穿衣服撐過冬天是巴索的奇蹟之一。他在市場和酒館附近出沒，教導慈愛。他是俄羅斯極少數敢批評恐怖伊凡的人之一。

❹ 離聖巴索只有幾步遠，位在紅場西側的是克里姆林宮。在俄文中，克里姆林是堡壘或城堡的意思。很多俄羅斯城鎮都有克里姆林。數百年來，紅場的克里姆林宮都是俄羅斯政治權力的中心。恐怖伊凡、凱薩琳女皇、列寧和史達林全都在克里姆林宮做過令人難忘的事。

❺ 就在克里姆林宮的外面，朝向紅場的北端，則有列寧之墓。假如你想看看列寧的遺體，只有一個地方可去，就是這裡了。弗拉基米爾·列寧是醉心工作的革命家，並成了蘇聯的首任領導人。從他在 1924 年過世以來，他的遺體就一直公開展示，生物結構研究所這個特殊機構則負責讓他保持美觀。

❻ 在列寧之墓前排隊的人龍不像過去那麼長了。很多人會直接一路走到國家歷史博物館，它就在克里姆林宮的北邊；或者更常走到俄羅斯最著名的古姆百貨賣場，它占據了紅場的整個東側。古姆百貨（唸法是「goom」）的全名是 *Glavnyi Universalnyi Magazin* ──「國家百貨公司」。想到柏帛麗、彪馬和卡文克萊，聖巴索大概不會有多大的興趣，但如今紅場的遊客就很少人抗拒得了去古姆百貨逛一下了。

🔑 精要句型

■ **A tour around the Red Square *works as* a crash course in Russian history.**

繞著紅場一遊，等於上了一堂俄羅斯歷史的速成課。

句型 **X works as Y.** 「X 等於 Y。」

當 X 有某種無法一目了然的用途或目的時，這個句型就很好用。用 Y 來說明 X。

例句 It's a fun movie, and it also *works as* an introduction to British politics.

這是部有趣的電影，它也等於在介紹英國的政治。

The geese outside my house *work as* an alarm system.

我屋子外面的鵝等於是警報系統。

📖 詞彙測驗

( ) **1.** The word **open** in paragraph 1, line 2 is closest in meaning to

    A. free

    B. clear

    C. large

    D. popular

( ) **2.** The word **right** in paragraph 5, line 1 is closest in meaning to

    A. opposite the left

    B. correct

    C. close by

    D. politically conservative

(　　) **3.** The phrase **makes up** in paragraph 6, line 4 is closest in meaning

to

A. applies cosmetics

B. catches up

C. forms

D. tells a lie

4. Underline the word in each group that doesn't belong.

a) tomb	cathedral	Red Square
b) Lenin	Stalin	Basil
c) Russia	Ivan the Terrible	Moscow
d) Tsar	Puma	King
e) center	north	line
f) visitor	leader	revolutionary

 旅 遊 一 點 通

在列寧之墓前，警察會上前調查表現得太過開心的遊客。遊客要是沒帶護照，有時候會被帶走盤查，並可能要繳交罰款。就算列寧不是你最喜愛的蘇聯人，在他的墓前也要畢恭畢敬。可以上這個網站進一步了解，當你去列寧之墓時，要怎麼表現才適當：

http://goeasteurope.about.com/od/russia/a/leninstomb.htm

旅遊好用句

可以照相嗎？找人問一下比較保險：

May I take pictures here?
「我可以在這裡拍照嗎？」

解 答

詞彙測驗

1. 第一段第二行中的「open」這個字最接近的意義是

A. 自由　B. 開闊無阻　C. 大　D. 普及

Ans　B

2. 第五段第一行中的「right」這個字最接近的意義是

A. 左邊的相反　B. 正確　C. 靠近　D. 政治保守

Ans　C

3. 第六段第四行中的「makes up」這個片語最接近的意義是

A. 化妝　B. 趕上　C. 構成　D. 撒謊

Ans　C

4. 用底線標示出各組中屬性不同的字。

a. 墓地　　　大教堂　　　紅場

b. 列寧　　　史達林　　　巴索

c. 俄羅斯　　恐怖伊凡　　莫斯科

d. 沙皇　　　彪馬　　　　國王

e. 中央　　　北邊　　　　列隊

f. 遊客　　　領導人　　　革命家

UNIT 8 | Hagia Sophia
聖索菲亞大教堂

Located in Turkey（土耳其）

❶ In the year 561 AD, a man named Procopius of Caesarea published a book about the buildings of the Roman Empire. In it he wrote about a church in Constantinople[1] that was so beautiful, people never got tired of looking at it. Each part of the church, he wrote, was in perfect harmony with all the other parts. Windows let the sunshine enter in a magical way, so that the building itself seemed to be producing light. That beautiful church was called Hagia Sophia.

❷ Hagia Sophia is Greek[2] for "holy wisdom." The Church of the Holy Wisdom of God (Hagia Sophia for short, or *Ayasofya* in Turkish[3]) was

built during the years 532-537 by the Roman Emperor[4] known as Justinian the Great. Being Emperor meant that when Justinian wanted something, nobody could tell him no, except maybe his wife Theodora—but that's another story. When

---

Ⓦ Ⓞ Ⓡ Ⓓ Ⓛ Ⓘ Ⓢ Ⓣ

1. Constantinople 〔ˌkɑnstæntəˋnopl〕 *n.* 君士坦丁堡（伊斯坦堡的舊名）
2. Greek 〔grɪk〕 *n.* 希臘語　*adj.* 希臘的
3. Turkish 〔ˋtɝkɪʃ〕 *n.* 土耳其語　*adj.* 土耳其的
4. emperor 〔ˋɛmpərə〕 *n.* 皇帝
5. column 〔ˋkɑləm〕 *n.* 柱；圓柱
6. embed 〔ɪmˋbɛd〕 *v.* 把……嵌入
7. crystal 〔ˋkrɪstl〕 *n.* 水晶
8. ton 〔tʌn〕 *n.* 噸；【口語】多量

he built Hagia Sophia, Justinian wanted something special, something very special, and he didn't care how much it cost. Columns[5] made of purple rock embedded[6] with crystals?[7] Yes. Tons[8] of black and white marble?[9] Yes. Gold-plated[10] ceilings? Yes. Giant mosaics[11] everywhere? Yes. Biggest church in the world? Yes.

❸ Hagia Sophia was designed by Isidore of Miletus and Anthemius of Tralles, architects who specialized[12] in physics and geometry.[13] Hagia Sophia's roof, its most famous feature, is a perfect dome.[14] Just underneath the dome, a row of arched windows runs all the way around the building. Sunlight pours in through these windows. Seen from within, the dome seems to float weightlessly[15] above the light-filled windows.

❹ Fast forward to the year 1453, when Constantinople is conquered[16] by

9. marble〔ˋmɑrb!〕*n.* 大理石
10. gold-plated〔ˋgoldˋpletɪd〕*adj.* 鍍金的
11. mosaic〔moˋze‧ɪk〕*n.* 馬賽克；馬賽克鑲嵌式之物
12. specialize〔ˋspɛʃəlaɪz〕*v.* 專攻
13. geometry〔dʒiˋɑmətrɪ〕*n.* 幾何學
14. dome〔dom〕*n.* (半球形的) 圓屋頂
15. weightlessly〔ˋwetlɪslɪ〕*adv.* 無重量地；無重力地
16. conquer〔ˋkɑŋkɚ〕*v.* 征服

Muslim Ottomans. Islamic[17] features like minarets[18] are added to Hagia Sophia, and Christian images inside the church are covered with white paint. It had been one of the most beautiful churches in the world. After a bit of redecorating, it became one of the world's most beautiful mosques.[19]

❺ Fast forward again, to the twentieth century. Constantinople is now known as Istanbul.[20] It's the capital[21] of Turkey, which became a modern nation under the leadership of Kemal Ataturk. He wanted to organize and rule the country according to non-religious ideas, so in 1935 he turned Hagia Sophia into a museum.

❻ Today, some Muslims[22] wish Hagia Sophia could be used once again as a mosque. Some Christians strongly object to that plan. Everybody agrees about one thing: Hagia Sophia is still beautiful. Today, almost fifteen hundred years after Procopius wrote his book, Hagia Sophia remains one of the most beautiful buildings in the world, and people still haven't gotten tired of looking at it.

Ⓦ Ⓞ Ⓡ Ⓓ Ⓛ Ⓘ Ⓢ Ⓣ

17. Islamic〔ɪsˋlæmɪk〕 *adj.* 伊斯蘭教的；回教的
18. minaret〔͵mɪnəˋrɛt〕 *n.* （回教寺院的）尖塔
19. mosque〔mɑsk〕 *n.* 清真寺；回教寺院
20. Istanbul〔͵ɪstɑnˋbul〕 *n.* 伊斯坦堡
21. capital〔ˋkæpətl〕 *n.* 首都
22. Muslim〔ˋmʌzlɪm〕 *n.* 回教徒

譯文

❶ 西元 561 年時,有個男子名叫凱撒里亞的普洛可比亞斯,他出版了一本書來談羅馬帝國的建築。在書中,他寫到君士坦丁堡有一座教堂十分美麗,令人百看不厭。他寫說,教堂的各個部分跟其他所有的部分都協調得很完美。窗戶讓陽光以奇妙的方式照射進來,因此建築物本身似乎就會發光。這座美麗的教堂就叫做聖索菲亞。

❷ 聖索菲亞在希臘文中是「神聖智慧」的意思。這座上帝神聖智慧的教堂(簡寫為聖索菲亞,或是土耳其文 *Ayasofya*)是在 532 到 537 年間,由被稱為查士丁尼大帝的羅馬皇帝所建造。當皇帝意謂著當查士丁尼想要什麼東西時,沒有人能對他說不,也許他太太希歐朵拉是個例外──但這是另外一回事。在建造聖索菲亞時,查士丁尼想要特別的東西,非常特別的東西,而且他不在乎要花多少錢。用鑲水晶的紫色岩石做成的圓柱?沒錯。一噸噸的黑白大理石?沒錯。鍍金的天花板?沒錯。到處都是巨大的馬賽克?沒錯。世界上最大的教堂?沒錯。

❸ 聖索菲亞是由建築師米利都的伊西多爾和特拉利茲的安西米厄斯所設計,他們專攻物理學與幾何學。聖索菲亞的屋頂是個完美的圓頂,並且是它最著名的特色。在圓頂正下方,一排拱形的窗子圍繞著整座建築物,陽光就從這些窗子灑進來。而從裡面看出去,圓頂似乎是不帶重量地漂浮在光芒四射的窗子上。

❹ 快轉來到 1453 年,當時君士坦丁堡被穆斯林的鄂圖曼人所征服。聖索菲亞增添了像尖塔這種伊斯蘭特色,教堂內的基督教圖案則用白漆蓋住。它原本是世界上最美麗的教堂之一。在重新裝潢一下後,它成了世界上最美麗的清真寺之一。

❺ 再次快轉來到 20 世紀。君士坦丁堡此時被稱為伊斯坦堡。它是土耳其的首都，在凱末爾的領導下，土耳其成了一個現代國家。他想要依照非宗教的觀念來組織及統治國家，於是在 1935 年，他把聖索菲亞改成了博物館。

❻ 如今有些穆斯林希望，聖索菲亞能再次當作清真寺。有些基督教徒則強烈反對這個計畫。大家都同意一件事：聖索菲亞還是很美。如今在普洛可比亞斯著書立作將近 1,500 年後，聖索菲亞依舊是世界上最美麗的建築之一，眾人對它還是百看不厭。

🔑 精要句型

■ **Hagia Sophia *is* Greek *for* "holy wisdom."**
聖索菲亞在希臘文中是「神聖智慧」的意思。

句型 **X is Y for Z.** 「在語言 Y 中，X 是 Z 的意思。」

例句 *Ay, caramba! is* Spanish *for* "Good grief!"
Ay, caramba! 在西班牙文中是「哎呀！」的意思。

Hakuna matata is Swahili *for* "No worries."
Hakuna matata 在斯瓦希里文中是「別擔心」的意思。

✏️ 詞彙測驗

( ) **1.** The word **harmony** in paragraph 1, line 7 is closest in meaning to

    A. structure   B. size

    C. balance   D. difficulty

( ) **2.** The word **architect** in paragraph 3, line 2 is closest in meaning to

    A. inventor   B. mathematician

    C. designer   D. physicist

( ) **3.** The word **rule** in paragraph 5, line 4 is closest in meaning to

    A. judge   B. law

    C. govern   D. consider

4. Underline the word in each group that doesn't belong.

    a) church   nation   mosque

    b) dome   column   gold-plated

c) Constantinople	Tralles	Istanbul
d) marble	crystals	mosaics
e) Procopius	Justinian	Kemal Ataturk
f) Theodora	Isidore	Anthemius

詞彙測驗

1. 第一段第七行中的「harmony」這個字最接近的意義是

A. 結構　B. 尺寸　C. 平衡　D. 困難

Ans C

2. 第三段第二行中的「architect」這個字最接近的意義是

A. 發明家　B. 數學家　C. 設計師　D. 物理學家

Ans C

3. 第五段第四行中的「rule」這個字最接近的意義是

A. 判斷　B. 法律　C. 治理　D. 考慮

Ans C

4. 用底線標示出各組中屬性不同的字。

a. 教堂	國家	清真寺
b. 圓頂	圓柱	鍍金
c. 君士坦丁堡	特拉利茲	伊斯坦堡
d. 大理石	水晶	馬賽克
e. 普洛可比亞斯	查士丁尼	凱末爾
f. 希歐朵拉	伊西多爾	安西米厄斯

UNIT
9 | **The Taj Mahal**
泰姬瑪哈陵

Located in India（印度）

❶ Everybody knows that people are never perfect. Can imperfect people make perfect things? Go see the Taj Mahal in Agra, India, and decide for yourself. If it's not perfect, it's close. The Taj Mahal has been described as a poem written with marble.[1] It is a love poem.

❷ Prince Khurram was the son of the Emperor of India. When he was fourteen years old, he fell in love with a princess. She was one year older and her name was Arjumand. Five years later, in the year 1612, Khurram and Arjumand were married. They went everywhere together and had many children. They were happy. In 1628, Khurram became Emperor of India. He took a new name: Shah Jahan. In Persian,[2] it means "King of the World." Shah Jahan gave his wife a new title too. He called her Mumtaz Mahal—"Jewel of the Palace." Twenty-one years after they first met, Shah Jahan and Mumtaz Mahal were still in love.

❸ Three years later, Mumtaz Mahal died after giving birth to the couple's

---

Ⓦⓞⓡⓓ Ⓛⓘⓢⓣ ──────────

1. marble 〔ˋmɑrbḷ〕 *n.* 大理石
2. Persian 〔ˋpɝʒən〕 *n.* 波斯語
3. spectacles 〔ˋspɛktəkḷz〕 *n.* (*pl.*) 眼鏡
4. crown 〔kraʊn〕 *n.* 王冠
5. geometry 〔dʒiˋɑmətrɪ〕 *n.* 幾何學
6. symmetrical 〔sɪˋmɛtrɪkḷ〕 *adj.* 左右對稱的；相稱的

fourteenth child. Shah Jahan was sick with sadness. As King of the World, he had many wives, but none of them could compare with his first love. Shah Jahan's beard turned gray. He had to start using spectacles.[3] One year after the death of his wife, Shah Jahan began constructing the Taj Mahal (Crown[4] Palace) as a tomb for her body. The basic geometry[5] of the Taj is simple and symmetrical.[6] The tomb is a large cube[7] with a domed[8] roof. At the four corners of the cube rise four slender minarets.[9] On each side of the cube, tall archways[10] frame arched doorways. Each part stands on its own while also playing a part in the overall design. Everything is made with white marble.

❹ Completed in 1653 after 22 years of labor by 22,000 workers, the Taj looks like it was created in Paradise, not on Earth. It is wondrously[11] beautiful. Some would say: perfect. Shah Jahan described it like this: "The sight of it creates sorrowing sighs; and the sun and the moon

---

7.　cube〔kjub〕 *n.* 立方體
8.　domed〔domd〕 *adj.* 半球形的；圓頂狀的
9.　minaret〔ˌmɪnəˋrɛt〕 *n.* 尖塔
10. archway〔ˋɑrtʃˌwe〕 *n.* 拱道；有拱門之入口
11. wondrously〔ˋwʌndrəslɪ〕 *adv.* 驚人地；不可思議地

shed[12] tears from their eyes."

❺ A few years later, Shah Jahan became weak with sickness. His sons began fighting each other. There were many battles and betrayals.[13] In the end the third son, Aurangzeb, was the winner. It was a bloody victory. Three of Aurangzeb's brothers had been captured[14] and murdered.

❻ Aurangzeb became the new Emperor. In 1659, he placed his father under house arrest.[15] From the window of his room, Shah Jahan could look out every day and see the Taj Mahal. He remained imprisoned[16] for five years, until his death in 1664. Shah Jahan is buried next to his wife in the Taj Mahal.

Ⓦⓞⓡⓓ Ⓛⓘⓢⓣ

12. shed 〔ʃɛd〕 v. 流出；滴下
13. betrayal 〔bɪˋtreəl〕 n. 背叛；出賣
14. capture 〔ˋkæptʃɚ〕 v. 逮捕；擄獲
15. under house arrest 軟禁
16. imprison 〔ɪmˋprɪzn〕 v. 禁閉

譯文

❶ 大家都知道，人絕非完美。不完美的人能不能做出完美的東西？去印度的阿格拉看看泰姬瑪哈陵，再自己判斷。它就算不完美，也相去不遠。泰姬瑪哈陵被形容為用大理石所寫成的詩，而且是首情詩。

❷ 胡拉姆親王是印度皇帝之子。在 14 歲時，他愛上了一位公主。她年長一歲，名叫阿柔曼。到了五年後的 1612 年，胡拉姆和阿柔曼結為連理。他們形影不離，並生了很多孩子。他們過得很快樂。1628 年時，胡拉姆當上了印度皇帝。他取了個新名字：沙・賈汗。在波斯文裡，它是「世界之王」的意思。沙・賈汗也為妻子取了個新頭銜。他稱她為蒙泰姬・瑪哈——「宮中珍寶」。在他們初識的 21 年後，沙・賈汗和蒙泰姬・瑪哈依舊相愛。

❸ 三年後，蒙泰姬・瑪哈因為生兩人的第 14 個孩子而過世。沙・賈汗也哀慟到生病。身為世界之王，他有好多個妻子，但沒有一個比得上他的初戀情人。沙・賈汗的鬍子白了，而且必須開始戴眼鏡。在妻子過世一年後，沙・賈汗開始興建泰姬瑪哈陵（皇冠宮殿），以埋葬她的遺體。泰姬的基本幾何學簡單而對稱。墓地是個大型的圓頂立方體，立方體的四個角則立了四根細長的尖塔。立方體的每一側都有高聳的拱門架構出拱形的出入口。每個環節自成一格，又在整體的設計中扮演了某種角色。每樣東西都是用白色大理石做成。

❹ 由 2 萬 2,000 個工人耗費 22 年的勞力，它在 1653 年完成了。泰姬看起來彷彿是建在天堂裡，而不是地球上。它美得令人讚歎。有的人會說：完美。沙・賈汗則是這麼描述它的：「看到它就令人悲嘆，日月的淚水都會從眼裡流下來。」

❺ 幾年後，沙‧賈汗因病而變得虛弱。他的兒子開始互鬥，戰爭與叛亂也頻頻發生。到最後，三子奧朗則布成了贏家。這是一場流血的勝利，奧朗則布有三個兄弟遭到了逮捕與殺害。

❻ 奧朗則布當上了新的皇帝。1659 年，他把父皇軟禁起來。透過房間的窗戶，沙‧賈汗每天都能往外看到泰姬瑪哈陵。他到 1664 年過世為止持續被關了五年。沙‧賈汗就葬在泰姬瑪哈陵裡妻子的旁邊。

精要句型

■ **The Taj Mahal *has been described as* a poem written with marble.**
泰姬瑪哈陵被形容為用大理石所寫成的詩。

句型 **X has been described as Y.** 「**X 被形容為 Y**。」

此句型常用來提出別人的陳述，某人是用 Y 來描述 X 的。但說話者不見得同意或不同意這項陳述。

例句 Counterterrorism agent Jack Bauer *has been described* by some *as* a hero and by others *as* a thug.
反恐隊員傑克‧包爾被某些人形容為英雄，也被某些人形容為惡棍。

The Circassian languages, spoken in the Cacasus Mountains, *have been described as* the world's most difficult to learn.
在高加索山區所說的索卡西亞語被形容為世上最難學。

詞彙測驗

一、**Translate each Chinese item by using words and phrases from the essay.**

    a) 取新名字   _____

    b) 哀慟到生病   _____

    c) 沒有一個比得上   _____

    d) 流下淚水   _____

    e) 流血的勝利   _____

    f) 軟禁   _____

二、**Underline the word in each group that doesn't belong.**

a) slender   large   cube

b) Agra   Emperor   Shah

c) house arrest   battle   imprisoned

d) marble   minaret   archway

e) Khurram   Aurangzeb   Arjumand

f) minaret   window   archway

解 答

詞彙測驗

一、利用文中的單字及片語來翻譯下列中文。

a) take a new name

b) sick with sadness

c) none can compare

d) shed tears

e) a bloody victory

f) under house arrest

二、用底線標示出各組中屬性不同的字。

a) 細長的 　　　大的 　　　立方體

b) 阿格拉 　　　皇帝 　　　沙

c) 軟禁的 　　　戰爭 　　　被關的

d) 大理石 　　　尖塔 　　　拱門

e) 胡拉姆 　　　奧朗則布 　　　阿柔曼

f) 尖塔 　　　窗 　　　拱門

UNIT 10 The Sydney Opera House
雪梨歌劇院

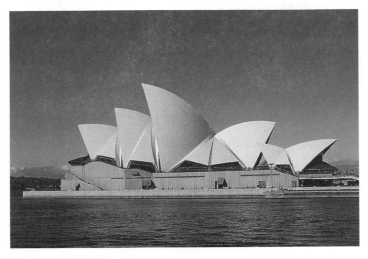

Located in Australia（澳洲）

❶ "Many people say my design was inspired by the sailing yachts[1] in the harbor," Jørn Utzon once told a reporter. The curving, rounded[2] segments of the Sydney Opera House *do* look like air-filled sails and

they *do* beautifully echo[3] the sails of the boats on the water in the harbor. Actually, though, the famous roof of the Opera House was inspired by—an orange.

❷ "It is like an orange," said Utzon, a Dane[4] who became the architect for the Opera House after winning a design competition in 1957. "You peel[5] an orange and you get these segments, these similar shapes."

The shell-like roof of the Opera House has fourteen segments. Put them all together: they form a perfect sphere.[6] For this reason, the building looks both complex and unified.[7]

❸ When construction began in 1959, the unique geometry[8] of Utzon's

---

ⓌⓄⓇⒹ ⓁⒾⓈⓉ

1. yacht 〔jɑt〕 *n.* 遊艇
2. rounded 〔ˋraʊndɪd〕 *adj.* 成圓形的；圓形隆起的
3. echo 〔ˋɛko〕 *v.* 反應；呼應
4. Dane 〔den〕 *n.* 丹麥人
5. peel 〔pil〕 *v.* 剝皮
6. sphere 〔sfɪr〕 *n.* 球形；球體

design posed enormous challenges to builders. One of the best engineers in the world, Ove Arup, helped figure out how to make it all possible. Unfortunately, in addition to the design and engineering difficulties, there were also political problems.

❹ While the Opera House was still under construction, a new government was elected in New South Wales, the Australian state where Sydney is located. The new Minister[9] for Public Works was Davis Hughes. Previously Hughes had been caught for lying about having a university degree, and he understood little about architecture or engineering. But he wanted to be in control of the Opera House.

❺ Hughes took control by criticizing and then refusing to pay Utzon. In 1966, unable to support his staff,[10] the architect was forced to quit the job. He left Australia and never returned. Work on the Opera House was completed by other architects. Many people believe the building (especially the interiors[11]) would have been even better if Utzon had been involved until the end. When the Opera House was completed in

7. unified〔`junəˌfaɪd〕adj. 一致的；統一的
8. geometry〔dʒi`amətrɪ〕n. 幾何學
9. minister〔`mɪnɪstə〕n. 大臣；部長
10. staff〔stæf〕n. 工作人員；成員
11. interior〔ɪn`tɪrɪə〕n. 內部

Unit 10 The Sydney Opera House 雪梨歌劇院 109

1973, Utzon was not invited to the opening ceremony.

❻ Eventually, many years later, the government of New South Wales made peace with Utzon. They asked him to redesign a room inside the Opera House and in 2004 it was named the Utzon Room in his honor. By then, Utzon was too old to travel back to Australia. He never saw the completed building. "But he lives and breathes the Opera House," said his son, "and as its creator he just has to close his eyes to see it."

❼ Today, the Opera House still looks daring[12] and modern. Universally recognized as a historic[13] masterpiece,[14] it is Australia's most famous, most iconic[15] building. "The sun did not know how beautiful its light was," said one admiring architect, "until it reflected off this building."

12. daring 〔ˋdɛrɪŋ〕 *adj.* 大膽的；嶄新的
13. historic 〔hɪsˋtɔrɪk〕 *adj.* 歷史上的；有歷史性的
14. masterpiece 〔ˋmæstɚ͵pis〕 *n.* 傑作；代表作
15. iconic 〔aɪˋkɑnɪk〕 *adj.* 偶像的；有代表性的

譯文

❶「有很多人說，我的設計是受到港內的遊艇所啓發。」約恩·烏特松曾經對記者說道。雪梨歌劇院彎曲的圓形切片看起來「的確」像是充滿氣的風帆，也「的確」美妙輝映了港內水上的船帆。但實際上，歌劇院著名的屋頂是受到「柳橙」所啓發。

❷「它就像個柳橙。」烏特松說。這位丹麥人在贏得 1957 年的設計比賽後，便成了歌劇院的建築師。「你把柳橙的皮剝開，就會得到這些切片，這些相似的形狀。」歌劇院貝殼狀的屋頂有 14 個切片。把它們全部拼起來，就能組成一個完美的球面。基於這個原因，這座建築看起來既複雜又有一致性。

❸ 當它在 1959 年開始施工時，烏特松所設計的獨特幾何學對建商造成了極大的挑戰。世界上最優秀的工程師之一歐甫·艾瑞甫幫忙想辦法把這一切化為可能。遺憾的是，除了設計和工程上的困難，還有政治上的問題。

❹ 歌劇院還在施工時，新南威爾斯選出了新政府，它是雪梨所在的澳洲省份。新任的公共工程部部長是戴維斯·休斯。過去休斯曾因謊稱擁有大學學位而遭人踢爆，而且他對建築或工程所知有限。但他卻想主管歌劇院。

❺ 休斯是靠批評來取得掌控，後來又拒絕付款給烏特松。到了 1966 年，由於無法養活工作團隊，建築師被迫離職。他離開了澳洲，再也沒有回來。歌劇院的工程是由其他的建築師所完成。很多人相信，假如烏特松能參與到最後，這座建築會更好（尤其是室內）。歌劇院在 1973 年完工時，烏特松並未受邀參加開幕典禮。

❻ 最後，經過了很多年，新南威爾斯政府才跟烏特松言歸於好。他們請他重

新設計歌劇院內部的一個廳室，並在 2004 年把它命名為烏特松廳，以向他致敬。當時烏特松已經太老而回不了澳洲。他從來沒有看過完工後的建築。「但他為歌劇院付出了一切。」他的兒子說。「而且身為它的創造者，他只需閉上眼睛就能看到它。」

❼ 如今歌劇院依然看起來既前衛又現代。它是公認的歷史傑作，也是澳洲最著名、最具代表性的建築。「太陽不會曉得它的光有多美。」有一位心懷崇敬的建築師說。「除非經過這座建築的反射。」

精要句型

■ He *lives and breathes* the Opera House.
他為歌劇院付出了一切。

句型 [Somebody] lives and breathes [something].
〔某人〕為〔某事〕付出了一切。

當你 live and breathe something 時，代表那件事對你十分重要。

例句 Jerry *lives and breathes* basketball. He even plays point guard in his dreams.
傑瑞為籃球付出了一切。他連在夢裡都在扮演控球後衛。

If you want to pass this test, you're going to have to *live and breathe* math for the next two months.
假如你想通過測驗，你就必須在接下來的兩個月為數學付出一切。

詞彙測驗

Match the words from the box to the speakers.

make peace	staff	architect	take control
admiration	complex		

_____ **1.** Can't we talk? I want to apologize for what I said before. Let's just start over again, OK? I want us to be friends.

_____ **2.** His specialty is designing bathrooms and he is really good at it. I wish I could live in one of his bathrooms.

3. This is hard. This is difficult. To be honest, I don't really get it. Can somebody please explain this to me?

4. I'd like you to meet Fred, Barney and Wilma. Without their smarts and hard work, this company would be nothing.

5. I'm in charge now. We're going to do things my way now. If you don't like it, get out.

6. Rain is my hero. He can sing and dance and do kung fu. His muscles are so muscular! And his epicanthic folded eyes are so sexy!

 旅 遊 一 點 通

體驗雪梨歌劇院有兩種方式：從外和從內。務必要兩者兼顧。當你在室內時，何不去看場表演？音樂廳是內部最大與最醒目的空間。可以上歌劇院的官方網頁去查查，當你去雪梨時，會有什麼節目：

http://www.sydneyoperahouse.com/

旅遊好用句

可以打電話到歌劇院詢問：

During the first week of February, what will be showing in the concert hall?

「在 2 月的第一週，音樂廳有什麼節目？」

詞彙測驗

把框框裡的字彙跟說話者配對。

1. make peace

譯文 我們不能談談嗎？我想要為我之前所說的話道歉。我們就重新開始，好嗎？我希望我們能當朋友。

2. architect

譯文 他的專長是設計浴室，而且他相當厲害。但願我能住在他的一間浴室裡。

3. complex

譯文 這很艱深。這很難。說實話，我不是很懂。能不能麻煩誰來跟我解釋一下？

4. staff

譯文 我要你見見弗瑞德、巴尼和威瑪。要是沒有他們的聰明和努力付出，這家公司就會一事無成。

5. take control

譯文 現在由我指揮。現在大家照我的方法來做事。假如你們不喜歡，那就滾蛋。

6. admiration

譯文 Rain 是我的英雄。他能歌善舞，還會功夫。他的肌肉真是發達！他的單眼皮真性感！

PART 3

歐洲

UNIT 11 | The Colosseum
羅馬競技場

Located in Italy（義大利）

❶ The Romans sure knew how to throw[1] a party. When the great amphitheater[2] known as the Colosseum was nearing[3] completion in the center of Rome, in the year 80 AD, the Emperor Titus launched[4] a celebration that lasted 100 days. It was a wild, popular, bloody spectacle.[5] Imagine a circus with all kinds of wild animals: lions, tigers and bears, crocodiles,[6] rhinos,[7] hippos, hyenas[8] and bulls, camels, elephants and ostriches.[9] Then imagine men with weapons, killing the animals—and each other. The ground within the arena[10] was covered with sand—in Latin, arena means "sand" and for the Romans the arena was the sandy place where the fighting happened. The sand was good for soaking[11] up all the blood. By the time the party was over, something like 2,000 men and 5,000 beasts were dead.

❷ The Colosseum could hold 50,000 spectators,[12] and was efficiently designed with 80 numbered entrances so that the entire crowd could enter, incredibly, in just fifteen minutes. Spectators used numbered tickets to find their seats (the numbers were printed on pieces of broken clay[13] pots). The Emperor and his family had the best seats. As

---

Ⓦⓞⓡⓓ Ⓛⓘⓢⓣ

1. throw〔θro〕v.【口語】舉辦（舞會等）
2. amphitheater〔ˋæmfəˌθiətə〕n.（古羅馬的）圓形露天劇場及競技場
3. near〔nɪr〕v. 接近；靠近
4. launch〔lɔntʃ〕v. 開始；著手
5. spectacle〔ˋspɛktək!〕n. 奇觀；大規模的場面
6. crocodile〔ˋkrɑkəˌdaɪl〕n. 鱷魚
7. rhino〔ˋraɪno〕n. 犀牛（= rhinoceros）
8. hyena〔haɪˋinə〕n. 土狼
9. ostrich〔ˋɔstrɪtʃ〕n. 鴕鳥

protection from the sun, a giant cloth awning[14] could be lifted above the crowds. Servants sprayed perfume against the stink[15] of the dead and dying. Food and drinks were served.

❸ If you've seen the movie *Gladiator*, you know how it worked. Many of the gladiators[16] who fought each other to the death were slaves or prisoners. Others fought for pay. Occasionally, the Emperor himself would

participate, but usually from the safety of a high platform.[17] In this way, Commodus (he was a model for the nasty[18] Emperor in *Gladiator*) apparently killed 100 lions in a single day. Another time, he proudly cut off the head of a running ostrich.

10. arena〔ə`rinə〕*n.*（古羅馬圓形劇場中央的）鬥技場；比武場

11. soak〔sok〕*v.* 吸入（液體）

12. spectator〔`spɛktetə〕*n.* 旁觀者

13. clay〔kle〕*n.* 黏土；泥土

14. awning〔`ɔnɪŋ〕*n.* 遮日篷；雨篷

15. stink〔stɪŋk〕*n.* 臭味；臭氣

16. gladiator〔`glædɪˌetə〕*n.*（古羅馬的）鬥劍者

17. platform〔`plætˌfɔrm〕*n.* 講台；台

18. nasty〔`næstɪ〕*adj.* 令人厭惡的；壞心眼的

❹ Today only about a third of the Colosseum is still standing. Fires and earthquakes destroyed some of it. Beginning in the 14th century, many stones were removed to make palaces and churches. Despite the damage, the Colosseum's high curving[19] walls and dozens of arched openings are still impressive. Nineteen centuries after it was built, it remains Rome's most famous, most iconic[20] building.

❺ Not everyone was a fan of the Colosseum. In the fourth century, a monk named Telemachus famously jumped down into the arena during a fight. "Please stop!" he cried out to the gladiators. At first, the crowd thought it was a joke. Then they realized that the monk was serious: he was trying to end their fun. They began throwing stones at Telemachus and did not stop until he was dead. Not long after that, in the year 404 AD, the Emperor Honorius banned[21] gladiator games from the Colosseum.

W O R D L I S T

19. curving〔ˋkɝvɪŋ〕 *adj.* 彎曲的
20. iconic〔aɪˋkɑnɪk〕 *adj.* 偶像的；具代表性的
21. ban〔bæn〕 *v.* 禁止

譯文

❶ 羅馬人肯定知道要怎麼辦派對。西元 80 年，被稱為羅馬競技場的大型露天劇場在羅馬的中心快要完工時，皇帝提多舉辦了持續 100 天的慶祝活動。它是個狂野、流行又血腥的奇景。試想在圓形的廣場上有著各式各樣的野生動物：獅子、老虎、熊、鱷魚、犀牛、河馬、土狼、公牛、駱駝、大象和鴕鳥。再試想有人拿著武器砍殺動物——以及彼此。競技場的地上鋪滿了沙子——在拉丁文中，「arena」即為「沙子」的意思。而對羅馬人來說，競技場則是舉行格鬥的沙地。沙子有助於把所有的血都吸乾。等到派對結束，大約死了 2,000 個人和 5,000 隻野獸。

❷ 羅馬競技場可以容納 5 萬個觀眾，並很有效率地設計了 80 個編號入口，使整個人群可以在不可思議的短短 15 分鐘內進場。觀眾是依編號的入場券來找位子（號碼是印在破陶罐的碎片上），皇帝和他的家人擁有最好的座位。為了遮陽，巨大的布篷可以架設在群眾上方。僕役會噴香水來去除已死和將死者的臭味，並有餐飲供應。

❸ 假如你看過《神鬼戰士》這部電影，你就知道它是怎麼回事。對打到死的戰士有很多都是奴隸或囚犯，有的人則是為賞金而戰。皇帝本人偶爾也會下場參加，但通常會有高台的安全措施。透過這種方式，康莫多斯（他就是《神鬼戰士》裡卑劣皇帝的原型）顯然可在一天殺掉 100 頭獅子。還有一次，他得意地砍下一隻奔跑鴕鳥的頭。

❹ 如今羅馬競技場大概只有三分之一仍然屹立。火災和地震摧毀了其中一部分。從 14 世紀開始，許多石頭被拆去蓋宮殿和教堂。儘管受到毀損，羅馬競技場的弧形牆壁和數十個拱形入口還是讓人印象深刻。建造完工的 19 個世紀後，它依然是羅馬最著名、最具代表性的建築。

❺ 並非人人都是羅馬競技場的粉絲。在第 4 世紀時，有一位叫做泰勒馬庫斯的修士在舉行格鬥時跳進了場中，並因此聲名大噪。「請住手！」他對著戰士大喊。起先群眾以為是在開玩笑，後來才發現，這位修士是來真的：他想要終止他們的玩樂。他們開始向泰勒馬庫斯丟石頭，直到他死了才罷手。此事過了不久，在西元 404 年時，皇帝霍諾里烏斯禁止了羅馬競技場的戰士競技。

精要句型

■ **By the time the party was over, *something like* 2,000 men and 5,000 beasts were dead.**

等到派對結束，大約死了 2,000 個人和 5,000 隻野獸。

句型 **... something like X ....** 「大約 X 個……」

「something like」常被用來指一個估計或大略的數目。

例句 I can't remember how many donuts I ate this morning—*something like* 12, or 15.

我記不得我今天早上吃了幾個甜甜圈——大概是 12 或 15 個。

Onno couldn't believe how many people had come to hear him sing. There must have been *something like* 5,000 people in the park.

小野不敢相信有這麼多人來聽他唱歌。公園裡一定有大約 5,000 個人。

詞彙測驗

Look at the words that go together with "fan" and use them to complete the sentences.

club		football
	fan	
loyal		let down

1. One of Jerry's goals in life is to become famous enough to have his own fan _____.

2. Nina is a huge _____ fan, but she can't stand to watch baseball, which she says puts her to sleep.

3. A _____ fan supports his or her team even during the bad times.

4. Prince Goofus' fans all felt _____ when he cancelled the concert.

旅 遊 一 點 通

羅馬的扒手非常厲害。他們可以拿走你的錢包、把錢抽走，再把錢包放回原位，而你還渾然不覺。羅馬競技場和威尼斯廣場（Piazza Venezia）之間的路叫做帝國廣場大道（Via dei Fori Imperiali），它尤其受遊客歡迎，所以也深受扒手歡迎。在那裡要小心，就算在人多擁擠的公車上也是一樣，其中有些還被稱爲「扒手快車」和「掉錢車」。

看看下列影片裡的好用秘訣，包括點咖啡、吃得便宜、在羅馬逛街，以及了解一下羅馬扒手最喜歡哪條公車路線：

http://www.youtube.com/watch?v=M37c8SBZVDU

旅遊好用句

假如有人碰你的腿，那可能是扒手在測試你的反應。你可以看他一眼，然後說：

Not today, friend.
「今天別想，朋友。」

解 答

詞彙測驗

請看看跟「fan」搭配使用的字，並用它們來完成句子。

1. club

譯文 傑瑞的人生目標之一是要變得夠有名，並擁有自己的粉絲會。

2. football

譯文 妮娜是個大足球迷，但卻受不了看棒球，因為她說那會讓她睡著。

3. loyal

譯文 忠心的球迷會支持自己的球隊，即使是在艱困的時刻。

4. let down

譯文 古弗斯王子的歌迷覺得很失望，因為他取消了演唱會。

UNIT 12 | **The Acropolis**
衛城

Located in Greece（希臘）

❶ The Acropolis is a rocky hill in Athens,[1] Greece where the ruins of a number of ancient buildings are located. Built around 2,500 years ago, these were the most important buildings in Athens at a time when Athens was becoming the most important city in the history of Western civilization.

❷ In the 5th century BC, Athens was a powerful city-state. Located on Greece's southern coast, the city was rich and had a strong navy. Athens was a center for education. Architecture and sculpture thrived[2] in the city. And Athens had a new form of government: democracy. During this time, Athens fielded[3] an all-star[4] team of great politicians, poets, historians, and philosophers.

❸ Most of the buildings on the Acropolis were built during this Athenian[5] Golden Age. The Parthenon,[6] the most famous, was a temple dedicated[7] to Athena[8]— the goddess for whom Athens is named. Although the building is largely in ruins, the giant columns

Ⓦⓞⓡⓓ Ⓛⓘⓢⓣ

1. Athens〔ˋæθɪnz〕 *n.* 雅典
2. thrive〔θraɪv〕 *v.* 繁榮；興盛；發跡
3. field〔fild〕 *v.* 組成
4. all-star〔ˋɔl͵stɑr〕 *adj.* 全是明星的；全是一流的
5. Athenian〔əˋθinɪən〕 *adj.* 雅典的
6. Parthenon〔ˋpɑrθə͵nɑn〕 *n.* 巴特農神殿

that form its outer walls are still standing.

❹ When they were new, the Parthenon and the other buildings of the Acropolis were painted in bright colors. Beautiful marble[9] and bronze[10] statues stood all around. The sculptures and carvings that decorated the buildings were

a high point of Greek art. Time, war, thieves, and modern pollution have destroyed much, but the ruins of the Acropolis still make an awesome impression. The Parthenon in particular remains stunning,[11] and over the years it has become a symbol that stands for the great accomplishments of the people of ancient Athens.

❺ Walking about the Acropolis, visitors are sometimes startled[12] to realize that they are seeing the same things Socrates saw, so many

---

7. dedicate〔`dɛdəˌket〕v. 供奉；奉獻
8. Athena〔ə`θinə〕n. 雅典娜
9. marble〔`mɑrbḷ〕n. 大理石
10. bronze〔brɑnz〕adj. 青銅製的
11. stunning〔`stʌnɪŋ〕adj.【口語】極漂亮的；絕色的
12. startle〔`stɑrtḷ〕v. 使驚嚇；使驚奇

years ago. When the Parthenon was completed in 432 BC, the great philosopher was 37 years old. He lived in Athens and spent his time teaching that the way to wisdom is to first realize how little you really know. On a slow day, he very possibly might have had a nap against one of those columns.

❻ In 432 BC, Herodotus was 52, busy writing his famous *Histories*—in the West, he is known as the Father of History. Sophocles was about 65, winning prizes for his tragic plays—2,500 years later, they are still greatly admired. Pericles was 63, working as a politician to perfect democracy in Athens—many people regard this system of government as one of humankind's greatest achievements.

❼ Everybody agrees that the Athenians got Western civilization off to a great start. Some have argued that the Greeks' achievements were not just a beginning but also a climax.[13] The great German writer Goethe was thinking of Athens in the 5th century BC when he wrote: "Of all peoples the Greeks have dreamt the dream of life best."

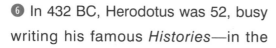

13. climax〔`klaɪmæks〕 *n.* 頂點；高峰

譯文

❶ 衛城是希臘雅典的一座岩山，有一些古建築的遺跡就在此地。它大約是在 2,500 年前所興建，當時雅典正成為西方文明史上最重要的城市，而它則是雅典最重要的建築。

❷ 在西元前 5 世紀，雅典是個強大的城邦。該城位於希臘的南岸，既富有又有強盛的海軍。雅典是個教育中心，城中的建築和雕塑也很興盛。雅典還擁有一個新的政府型態：民主。在這段時期，雅典出現了明星級陣容的偉大政治家、詩人、歷史家與哲學家。

❸ 衛城的建築大部分都是在雅典的這段黃金時期所興建。最著名的巴特農神廟是供奉雅典娜的廟宇，而雅典就是得名自這位女神。雖然這座建築多半已成為廢墟，但構成外牆的巨大圓柱依然挺立。

❹ 在嶄新的時候，巴特農神廟和衛城的其他建築被漆上鮮豔的色彩，而且到處樹立著美麗的大理石與青銅雕像。建築上所裝飾的雕塑與雕刻則是希臘藝術的高峰。歲月、戰爭、盜竊和現代污染造成不少破壞，但衛城的遺跡依然令人驚豔。尤其巴特農神廟還是令人讚歎，長年下來也成了代表古雅典人民偉大成就的象徵。

❺ 在衛城遊走，遊客有時候會驚訝地發現，自己正看著蘇格拉底在許許多多年前所看的相同東西。當巴特農神廟在西元前 432 年完成時，這位偉大的哲學家是 37 歲。他住在雅典，並花時間教導大家，通往智慧的道路就是先認清自己真正懂的東西有多微不足道。在某個悠閒的日子裡，他非常有可能曾靠在其中一根圓柱上打盹。

❻ 西元前 432 年時，希羅多德是 52 歲，正忙著寫他著名的《歷史》——在西方，他被稱為歷史之父。索福克勒斯是 65 歲左右，靠著他的悲劇贏得了獎項——2,500 年後，它們依然備受推崇。伯里克利是 63 歲，擔任政治家，以精進雅典的民主——有許多人把這套政體視為人類最偉大的成就之一。

❼ 大家都同意，雅典人為西方文明的開始帶來了好的起點。有的人認為，希臘人的成就不但是起步，更是個頂點。偉大的德國作家歌德在想到西元前 5 世紀的雅典人時寫道：「在所有的民族中，最懂得作人生大夢的就是希臘人。」

 **精要句型**

■ *Of all* peoples the Greeks have dreamt the dream of life *best*.
在所有的民族中，最懂得作人生大夢的就是希臘人。

句型 **Of all Xs [X¹, X², X³, etc.] the best/worst/scariest/etc. is Xʸ.**

「在所有的 **Xs**〔**X¹**、**X²**、**X³** 等等〕中，最會 / 最不會 / 最膽小……的就是 **Xʸ**。」

此句型可用來說明，某個項目在一大群相關項目中很突出。

例句 *Of all* the places described in this book, Dave *most* wants to visit the Alhambra.
在這本書所描述的地方中，戴夫最想造訪阿蘭布拉宮。

Of all actresses, isn't Chloë Sevigny *the coolest*?
在所有的女演員中，可蘿‧塞維尼可不是最酷的嗎？

詞彙測驗

Look at the words that go together with "wisdom" and use them to complete the sentences.

source of	popular
wisdom	
seeking	words of

1. Beth went to India _____ wisdom and enlightenment and she found loneliness and diarrhea.

2. If you really need to finish that paper tonight, I have three _____ wisdom for you: drink more coffee.

3. According to _____ wisdom, the best things in life are free.

4. Professor Wickliff believes Plato's dialogues are the world's greatest _____ wisdom. To make him mad, his wife Lindsay says that "The Simpsons" is even wiser.

旅 遊 一 點 通

雅典最古老的街道是阿德連街（Adrianou Street），民眾在上面走了幾千年。它通往歷史悠久的普拉卡（Plaka）地區，而衛城就在隔壁。普拉卡到處都是迷人的狹窄街道，林立著博物館、旅館、奇特的商店、夜店和咖啡店。你可以試試茴香烈酒，它是希臘最著名的甘草味酒飲。找個合適的地方，你就能坐在戶外欣賞衛城高處巴特農神廟的景色。它在夜晚發亮時，看起來特別美。可以利用下列網頁研究普拉卡地區的地圖：

http://www.planetware.com/map/athens-plaka-map-gr-plak.htm

旅遊好用句

假如你願意多花一點錢，你也可以弄個視野很棒的旅館房間來住：

If possible, I'd like a room with a view. Do you have any with views of the Parthenon?

「假如可能的話，我想要有景觀的房間。你們有沒有什麼房間可以看到巴特農神廟？」

詞彙測驗

請看看跟「wisdom」搭配使用的字,並用它們來完成句子。

1. seeking

譯文 貝絲去印度尋求智慧與啓蒙,得到的卻是孤單與腹瀉。

2. words of

譯文 假如你真的要在今天晚上把論文完成,那我送你一句智慧之言:咖啡多喝點。

3. popular

譯文 根據民間智慧,生命中最美好的事物是免費的。

4. source of

譯文 威克里夫教授相信,柏拉圖的言論是世界上最棒的智慧來源。為了氣他,他太太琳賽說,《辛普森家庭》更是睿智。

UNIT 13 | The Alhambra
阿蘭布拉宮

Located in Spain（西班牙）

❶ Be honest: how long can you really enjoy yourself in a museum or at a monument?¹ It's on the tour, it's on the list, so you go. Then, after about twenty minutes, or maybe an hour if you've had a lot of practice, you're ready to escape. The Alhambra is different. It's a world-famous monument, a palace-fortress² built for kings. Yet it is so pleasant, so lovely, and so peaceful, you are in no hurry to leave. It's so nice, you might even wish you could stay permanently³ and live there.

❷ The Alhambra is a group of buildings located atop⁴ a hill in Granada, Spain. First and foremost⁵ is the palace built during the 14th century by the Moorish⁶ rulers of Granada. The Moors⁷ were Muslims⁸  from North Africa who conquered the Iberian Peninsula (Spain and Portugal) early in the 8th century and remained for nearly 800 years. There are many Moorish buildings in Spain. Alhambra is the most famous.

Ⓦ Ⓞ Ⓡ Ⓓ Ⓛ Ⓘ Ⓢ Ⓣ

1. monument 〔`mɑnjəmənt〕 *n.* 紀念碑；紀念建築物
2. fortress 〔`fɔrtrɪs〕 *n.* 要塞；堅固的場所
3. permanently 〔`pɜmənəntlɪ〕 *adv.* 永久地
4. atop 〔ə`tɑp〕 *prep.* 在……上面；在……頂上
5. foremost 〔`for‚most〕 *adj.* 最前的；最先的；主要的
6. Moorish 〔`mʊrɪʃ〕 *adj.* 摩爾人的
7. Moor 〔mʊr〕 *n.* 摩爾人
8. Muslim 〔`mʌzlɪm〕 *n.* 回教徒
9. inviting 〔ɪn`vaɪtɪŋ〕 *adj.* 誘惑人的；讓人心動的
10. homey 〔`homɪ〕 *adj.* 像家一樣的

❸ The outside walls of the Alhambra are a plain, humble brown. Despite its great size, the complex looks inviting[9] and comfortable, even homey.[10] Simultaneously[11] simple and ornate,[12] designed to welcome the breeze and the sunlight, with interior surfaces dense[13] with decoration, the palace is a charming maze[14] of rooms and courtyards[15] and gardens.

❹ Islamic[16] architecture favors geometric[17] patterns known as arabesques.[18] On floors, walls, ceilings and doorways, painted and carved, these patterns are repeated throughout the palace and grounds. Many of the patterns are based on Arabic script and verses[19] from

Islam's holy book, the Koran.[20] The god of Islam is known as Allah, and this word appears in Arabic thousands of times within the palace.

❺ Each color used within the Alhambra has a special meaning, based

11. simultaneously〔ˌsaɪml`tenɪəslɪ〕 adv. 同時地
12. ornate〔ɔr`net〕 adj. 裝飾華麗的
13. dense〔dɛns〕 adj. 密集的
14. maze〔mez〕 n. 迷宮
15. courtyard〔`kort͵jɑrd〕 n. 中庭；庭院
16. Islamic〔ɪs`læmɪk〕 adj. 回教的；伊斯蘭教的
17. geometric〔ˌdʒiə`mɛtrɪk〕 adj. 幾何的；幾何學圖形的
18. arabesque〔ˌærə`bɛsk〕 n. 阿拉伯式圖案
19. verse〔vɝs〕 n. 韻文；詩歌
20. Koran〔ko`ræn〕 n. 可蘭經

on the teachings in the Koran. Red stands for blood, blue for heaven. Golden yellow means wealth. Oases[21] are symbolized by green. Water is everywhere within Alhambra, in reflective[22] pools and cascading[23] fountains and streams running through the gardens. The Moors came from dry places where water was precious. To them, water meant life.

❻ The Moors planted their gardens with roses and orange trees and hedges[24] of myrtle.[25] The elms[26] and cypresses[27] that have grown up since are filled with songbirds,[28] including the nightingales that sing even when the moon is up. At Alhambra, looking through an arched doorway out into a sunny green garden, admiring the colors of the wildflowers reflected in a quiet pool of water, listening to the songbirds, you can't help but feel a bit envious of those long gone Moorish princes. Living at Alhambra, they sure had it good.

ⓌⓄⓇⒹ ⓁⒾⓈⓉ

21. oases〔oˋesiz〕*n.* (oasis 的複數型) 綠洲
22. reflective〔rɪˋflɛtɪv〕*adj.* 反射的
23. cascade〔kæsˋked〕*v.* 像瀑布般落下
24. hedge〔hɛdʒ〕*n.* 樹籬
25. myrtle〔ˋmɝtl̩〕*n.* 桃金孃（一種蔓生之夾竹桃科長春草屬植物）
26. elm〔ɛlm〕*n.* 榆樹
27. cypress〔ˋsaɪprəs〕*n.* 柏樹
28. songbird〔ˋsɔŋˏbɝd〕*n.* 鳴禽；鳴鳥

譯文

❶ 說實話，你可以津津有味地待在博物館或紀念館裡多久？它在行程裡，它在清單上，於是你就去了。接著過了 20 分鐘左右，如果你練習過很多次也許可待到一小時，你就準備要開溜了。阿蘭布拉宮不一樣。它是舉世聞名的紀念館，一座為國王所興建的宮殿式堡壘。但它十分宜人、十分優美，也十分寧靜，所以你不會急著離開。它好得不得了，你甚至可能希望自己能永遠留下來並「住」在那裡。

❷ 阿蘭布拉宮是一群位在西班牙格拉納達山頂的建築。首要之處在於，這座宮殿是在 14 世紀時由統治格拉納達的摩爾人所興建。摩爾人是來自北非的穆斯林，他們在 8 世紀初征服了伊比利半島（西班牙和葡萄牙），並維持了將近 800 年。西班牙留有許多摩爾人的建築，最著名的就是阿蘭布拉宮。

❸ 阿蘭布拉宮的外牆是樸實無華的棕色。儘管占地很大，但整個園區看起來讓人心動又舒適，甚至有家的感覺。它兼具了簡單與富麗，在設計上可引入微風與日光，內部的外觀則布滿了裝飾。宮殿像是由廳房、庭院和花園組成的一座迷人迷宮。

❹ 伊斯蘭建築偏好所謂阿拉伯花紋的幾何圖案。在地板、牆壁、天花板和門廊上，有畫的也有刻的，這些圖案反覆出現在整個宮殿與地面。許多圖案裡的阿拉伯文字與詩文是取自伊斯蘭的聖經可蘭經。伊斯蘭的神名為阿拉，這個字的阿拉伯文在宮殿裡出現了成千上萬次。

❺ 阿蘭布拉宮裡的顏色各有特殊的意義，並且是以可蘭經的教義為依據。紅色代表血，藍色代表天國。金黃色是財富的意思，綠色則象徵了綠洲。阿蘭

布拉宮到處都是水，包括映象池、噴泉，以及流經花園的溪水。摩爾人是來自水很珍貴的乾燥地區。所以對他們來說，水就代表了生命。

❻ 摩爾人在花園裡種了玫瑰和柳橙樹，並以香桃木作為圍籬。後來所長出來的榆樹和柏樹則布滿了鳴鳥，其中包含了連在月亮升起時都會唱歌的夜鶯。在阿蘭布拉宮，透過拱形門廊往外看著陽光普照的綠色花園，欣賞野花映照在平靜水池裡的顏色，聽著鳥兒歌唱，你不禁會覺得有點羨慕這些過往已久的摩爾王族。住在阿蘭布拉宮裡，他們肯定很愜意。

精要句型

■ *It's so* nice, *you might* even wish you could stay permanently and live there.

它好得不得了，你甚至可能希望自己能永遠留下來並住在那裡。

句型 It's so X, you might Y. 「它很……，你可能會……。」

某事──或人、地、物──有 X 的特質。由於這種特質極為顯著，所以導致了 Y。Y 是 X 的結果。另一個常用的類似句型為：Somebody is so X, he or she ... Y.

例句 Be careful when you chop those peppers! *They're so* hot, *you might* burn your hands.

你在剁這些椒的時候要小心！它們辣得不得了，你可能會辣到自己的手。

You're so lazy, *you probably* won't even read all the way to the end of this sentence.

你懶得不得了，你甚至可能不會把這句話從頭念到尾。

詞彙測驗

( ) **1.** Which of the following definitions of **favors** describes how the word is used in paragraph 4, line 1?

A. acts of assistance

B. give an advantage to somebody or something

C. small gifts given to guests at a party

D. have a tendency to do things a certain way

( ) **2.** Which of the following definitions of **running** describes how the word is used in paragraph 5, line 7?

A. to be turned on and working

B. to move fast using feet

C. to pass from one place to another

D. to control a project or an operation

(　　) **3.** Which of the following definitions of **a bit** describes how the phrase is used in paragraph 6, line 9?

A. a unit of information

B. a wound caused by teeth

C. a small amount of something

D. a tool for drilling holes

 旅 遊 一 點 通

有時候阿蘭布拉宮會非常忙，每天多達 8,000 人來參訪。為了確保自己去格拉納達時能看到宮殿，不妨事前預約。阿蘭布拉宮的淡季是冬天以及 7、8 月（因為格拉納達會非常熱）。避開人群的另一種方法是在晚上去。（晚上你不能逛完整個園區，但可以看到宮殿，它在夜幕中很漂亮。）上網訂票可至下列網站：

http://www.alhambra-tickets.es/

旅遊好用句

假如你已經事先訂了票，可以在抵達時告訴他們：

I have reserved tickets, under the name Constance Noring.

「我有訂票，名字是 Constance Noring。」

解 答

詞彙測驗

1. 在「favors」的下列定義中，哪一個是在描述這個字在第四段第一行中的用法？

A. 援助行動

B. 使某人或某物占有優勢

C. 在宴會上給來賓的小禮物

D. 傾向以特定的方式來做事

Ans D

2. 在「running」的下列定義中，哪一個是在描述這個字在第五段第七行中的用法？

A. 啟動並開始作業

B. 用腳快速移動

C. 從一地移到另一地

D. 掌控專案或運作

Ans C

3. 在「a bit」的下列定義中，哪一個是在描述這個詞在第六段第九行中的用法？

A. 資訊的單位

B. 牙齒所造成的傷口

C. 少量的某種東西

D. 鑽孔的工具

Ans C

The Eiffel Tower
艾菲爾鐵塔

Located in France

（法國）

❶ Are there any French people who *don't* like the Eiffel Tower? There used to be at least one. He was a famous writer and his name was Guy de Maupassant. He hated the Eiffel Tower. He hated it so much that he frequently went there for lunch, in a restaurant high up in the Tower itself. The food wasn't anything special. No—he ate there because while he was *inside* the Tower, he wouldn't have to *look* at it.

❷ At 324 meters, the Eiffel Tower was, and still is, the tallest structure in Paris. Built for the 1889 World's Fair and named after Gustave Eiffel, the man who designed and engineered[1] it, the Tower was essentially meant to be a giant tourist attraction.[2] It worked. Since it first opened, more than 200 million people have visited.

❸ The Tower is made of 18,000 pieces of iron, all attached[3] together in an open framework.[4] (Worried about the wind, Eiffel decided to let it blow right through the tower.) Seen up close, the iron pieces make crisscross[5] patterns

1. engineer 〔ˌɛndʒəˋnɪr〕 *v.* 監督工程；設計工程
2. tourist attraction 〔ˋturɪst əˋtræʃən〕 *n.* 觀光勝地
3. attach 〔əˋtætʃ〕 *v.* 附著；裝；黏
4. framework 〔ˋfremˌwɜk〕 *n.* 框架
5. crisscross 〔ˋkrɪsˌkrɔs〕 *n.* 十字形；交叉
6. solid 〔ˋsɑlɪd〕 *adj.* 實心的
7. spear 〔spɛr〕 *v.* （以尖物）刺

that most people, unlike Maupassant, find graceful. Seen from a distance, the tower appears as a solid,[6] straight line that spears[7] into the sky, a sight which most people, unlike Maupassant, find impressive.

❹ At some point, the Eiffel Tower graduated from tourist attraction to universal symbol. Nowadays, it is recognized everywhere as a symbol for Paris, and for France. Almost everybody who travels to Paris for the first time already has an image of the Eiffel Tower in his or her mind's eye. How do people know what it looks like if they've never seen it? Oh, they've seen it, and so have you. The Eiffel Tower has been duplicated[8] so often, it is almost impossible to avoid it. The Tower appears over and over again in movies and on postcards, in snow globes,[9] on key chains,[10] as salt and pepper shakers,[11] and on travel posters.[12]

❺ So far, nobody has built a copy of the Eiffel Tower bigger than the original, but replicas[13] of varying sizes can be found all around the world: in front of a casino in Las Vegas; at a theme park in Shenzhen, China; working as a cell phone tower in Chelyabinsk Oblast, Russia; in a shopping mall in Malaysia; on the roof of a factory in Satteldorf,

---

8. duplicate〔ˈdjupləˌket〕v. 複製
9. snow globe〔ˈsnoˌglob〕n. 雪花球
10. key chain〔ˈkiˌtʃen〕n. 鑰匙圈
11. salt and pepper shaker〔ˈsɔltˌəndˈpɛpɚˈʃekɚ〕n. 椒鹽罐
12. poster〔ˈpostɚ〕n. 海報
13. replica〔ˈrɛplɪkə〕n. 複製品

Germany; in Paris, Michigan; in Paris, Texas; at a resort[14] in Bulgaria; at an oil company in Kazakhstan; and just for the heck of it in many other places.

6 Imagine how poor Maupassant would feel if he were alive today. There would be no place in the world for him to hide. Or rather, just the one place, where he'd probably be eating three meals a day.

Ⓦ Ⓞ Ⓡ Ⓓ Ⓛ Ⓘ Ⓢ Ⓣ

14. resort〔rɪˋzɔrt〕 *n.* 休閒勝地

譯文

❶ 有沒有哪個法國人「不」喜歡艾菲爾鐵塔？起碼有過一個。他是個知名作家，名字叫做居伊・德・莫泊桑。他討厭艾菲爾鐵塔，討厭得不得了，所以經常去那裡吃午餐，餐廳就高懸在鐵塔上面。菜色一點都不特別，真的──他到那裡用餐是因為當他身在鐵塔「裡面」，就不必「看到」它了。

❷ 324 公尺的艾菲爾鐵塔曾經而且仍然是巴黎最高的結構體。它是為了 1889 年的世界博覽會所興建，並以設計與監造它的人古斯塔夫・艾菲爾來命名。這座鐵塔基本上是用來作為大型的觀光景點，效果很好。打從它首次開放以來，已有 2 億多人去參觀過。

❸ 該塔用了 1 萬 8,000 塊鐵打造而成，全部組裝在一座開放式的骨架。（由於擔心風勢，艾菲爾決定讓風直接穿透鐵塔。）靠近往上看，鐵條是呈現十字形圖案。不像莫泊桑，大部分人都覺得很優美。拉遠來看，該塔是一實心直線，直指天際。不像莫泊桑，大部分人看了都覺得印象深刻。

❹ 在某個時間點，艾菲爾鐵塔從觀光勝地晉升成為舉世皆知的象徵。現在，它在各地都被視為巴黎與法國的象徵。幾乎每個第一次去巴黎旅遊的人，腦海裡都已經對艾菲爾鐵塔有印象。如果從來沒看過，大家怎麼會知道它長什麼樣子呢？哦，他們都看過，你也是。艾菲爾鐵塔如此常被拿來複製，幾乎忽視不了它。鐵塔一而再地出現在電影和明信片、雪花球、鑰匙圈、椒鹽罐，以及旅遊海報。

❺ 到目前為止，還沒有人仿製過比本尊還大的艾菲爾鐵塔，但在世界各地都可以找到不同尺寸的複製品：在拉斯維加斯的賭場前面；在中國深圳的主題公園裡；在俄羅斯的車里雅賓斯克州化身為行動電話的基地台；在馬來西亞

的大賣場裡；在德國薩特朵夫的工廠屋頂上；在密西根州的巴黎；在德州的巴黎；在保加利亞的休閒勝地；在哈薩克的石油公司裡；以及其他許多莫名其妙的地方。

❻ 想像一下，假如可憐的莫泊桑活在現代，他會覺得如何。他在這個世界上將無容身之處。或者說只有一個地方，而且他大概一天三餐都要在那裡吃了。

 **精要句型**

■ **Replicas of the Eiffel Tower have been built *just for the heck of it*, all around the world.**

世界各地都有人沒來由地在做艾菲爾鐵塔的複製品。

句型 **... for the heck of it ...** 「……沒來由地……」

「To do something for the heck of it」是指缺乏好的理由去做某事，而只是因為你想做。Heck 是 hell 比較婉轉的用字。如果你想的話，你也可以做某事 for the hell of it。

例句 *Just for the heck of it*, Cecilia and Michelle decided to wear everything pink on Friday.

塞西莉亞和蜜雪兒沒來由地決定在星期五穿得一身粉紅。

A-Wei was bored. *Just for the heck of it*, he decided to buy a goat.

阿偉真無聊。他沒來由地決定去買一頭羊。

詞彙測驗

Look at the words that go together with "symbol" and use them to complete the sentences.

status		universal
	symbol	
for		sex

1. The Eiffel Tower is a symbol _____ France.

2. If you want to be a successful pop singer, it helps to look like a _____ symbol.

3. Is the human skull a _____ symbol for death?

4. Want a _____ symbol? Buy a yacht.

 旅 遊 一 點 通

假如你有懼高症，艾菲爾鐵塔可能會很嚇人。遊客可以爬階梯到鐵塔的第一和第二層。第二層要走 674 階才會到。過了那裡後，還要走 1,036 階才會到塔頂，但這部分並不對外開放，你必須搭電梯才行。（頭兩層也有電梯可搭。）該塔是開放式結構，而不是封閉式建築，所以不管是走階梯還是搭電梯，你都可以清楚看到及感覺到自己有多高。詳情可上艾菲爾鐵塔的官方網站查詢：

http://www.tour-eiffel.fr/teiffel/uk/

旅遊好用句

想要確認自己不是跟在前往爬樓梯的人群後面，可以問：

Is this the line for the stairs, or for the elevator?

「這一行人是排往階梯還是電梯？」

詞彙測驗

請看看跟「symbol」搭配使用的字，並用它們來完成句子。

1. for

　譯文 艾菲爾鐵塔是巴黎的象徵。

2. sex

　譯文 假如你想當個成功的流行歌手，看起來像個性感象徵會有所幫助。

3. universal

　譯文 人的頭骨是舉世皆知的死亡象徵嗎？

4. status

　譯文 想要地位的象徵嗎？買艘遊艇吧。

Neuschwanstein
新天鵝堡

Located in Germany（德國）

❶ Neuschwanstein Castle in Germany looks just like you expect a castle to look. Surrounded by dark pine[1] trees, with mountains in the background, the castle—it's also a palace—sits atop[2] a steep rocky hill above a lake. The high castle walls and all the many spires[3] and turrets[4] glow white under the sun. When you first see Neuschwanstein (German for "New Swan Stone"), you may wonder: Am I in a fairy tale?

❷ Before it became one of the most popular attractions in Germany and the inspiration[5] for Walt Disney's Sleeping Beauty Castle, Neuschwanstein was the fantasy[6] of King Ludwig II of Bavaria. Ludwig started designing the castle in 1869. Rather than consult with an architect, he first worked with a stage designer—the person who creates the fantastic[7] settings[8] for ballets, plays and operas. King Ludwig loved the music of Richard Wagner, one of the greatest composers of the 19th century. The king imagined his castle as a tribute[9] to Wagner. Like Wagner's music, the

---

Ⓦ Ⓞ Ⓡ Ⓓ Ⓛ Ⓘ Ⓢ Ⓣ

1. pine〔paɪn〕 *n.* 松木
2. atop〔əˋtɑp〕 *prep.* 在……頂上；在……上面
3. spire〔spaɪr〕 *n.* 尖塔；尖峰
4. turret〔ˋtɝɪt〕 *n.* 角塔；塔樓；砲塔
5. inspiration〔͵ɪnspəˋreʃən〕 *n.* 靈感；啓發
6. fantasy〔ˋfæntəsɪ〕 *n.* 想像；幻想
7. fantastic〔fænˋtæstɪk〕 *adj.* 【口語】極好的；很棒的
8. setting〔ˋsɛtɪŋ〕 *n.* 布景；背景

castle would be romantic, dramatic[10] and larger-than-life. (Some have said that in order to pay proper tribute to Wagner's ego,[11] the castle should have been even bigger.)

❸ Neuschwanstein is nothing if not dramatic, and not just from the outside. Inside, the walls are covered with giant paintings, showing scenes from Wagner's operas and German legends. Winding[12] staircases[13] disappear into towers. A gold chandelier[14] hangs from a ceiling. It took fourteen men almost five years just to carve[15] the wood in Ludwig's bedroom.

❹ Building fantasies isn't cheap. By 1885, after having spent all his money on various palaces and castles, Ludwig was 14 million marks[16] in debt. Neuschwanstein was still not finished, and Ludwig wanted to borrow more

9. tribute〔`trɪbjut〕 *n.* 貢物;(表示敬意的)讚辭
10. dramatic〔drə`mætɪk〕 *adj.* 戲劇性的;激動人心的
11. ego〔`igo〕 *n.*【口語】自大;自尊心
12. winding〔`waɪndɪŋ〕 *adj.* 螺旋狀的
13. staircase〔`stɛr͵kes〕 *n.*(包括扶手欄杆的)樓梯
14. chandelier〔͵ʃændḷ`ɪr〕 *n.* 枝形吊燈
15. carve〔kɑrv〕 *v.* 雕刻
16. mark〔mɑrk〕 *n.*【德國的貨幣單位】馬克

money. King Ludwig's ministers[17] decided that they had to stop him. Four doctors signed a report declaring the king insane. "How can you declare me insane?" complained Ludwig. "After all, you have never seen or examined me before!" Despite his protests,[18] Ludwig was removed from power. Less than a week later he was found floating in a lake, dead. The water was shallow.[19] King Ludwig was known to be a good swimmer. His death remains a mystery to this day.

⑤ In 1886, seven weeks after Ludwig's death, Neuschwanstein Castle was opened to visitors. The government's financial ministers needed to raise some money. In the years since, Neuschwanstein has become one of Europe's most famous buildings. Millions of tourists visit Germany to see this perfect fairy tale castle, which comes, like a good fairy tale should, complete with its own dark secrets. Through the years, Ludwig's Neuschwanstein Castle has earned enough money to pay for itself over and over again.

Ⓦ Ⓞ Ⓡ Ⓓ   Ⓛ Ⓘ Ⓢ Ⓣ

17. minister 〔`mɪnɪstə〕 *n.* 大臣；部長
18. protest 〔`protɛst〕 *n.* 抗議
19. shallow 〔`ʃælo〕 *adj.* 淺的

譯文

❶ 德國的新天鵝堡看起來就像你所期望的城堡外觀一樣。四周是深色的松樹，背倚著山脈。這座城堡，也是個宮殿，位在一座陡峭岩丘的頂端，底下則有一座湖。城堡的高牆、以及許許多多的尖塔和角塔，全都在陽光下閃閃發亮。當你第一次看到新天鵝堡時（德文的意思是「新天鵝石」），你可能會懷疑：我是不是到了童話世界裡？

❷ 在成為德國最受歡迎的勝地之一，以及華德‧迪士尼睡美人城堡的靈感前，新天鵝堡是巴伐利亞路德維希二世國王的夢想。路德維希在 1869 年開始設計城堡。他並沒有請教建築師，而是先和舞台設計師合作。此設計師為芭蕾、舞台劇、歌劇創造了很棒的布景。路德維希國王喜愛理查‧華格納的音樂，他是 19 世紀最偉大的作曲家之一。國王把他的城堡想成是獻給華格納的貢物。就跟華格納的音樂一樣，這座城堡應該是浪漫、充滿戲劇性、超越平凡的。（有人曾說，要適切表達對華格納自大的敬意，城堡應該還要再更大。）

❸ 新天鵝堡十分具有戲劇性，而且不只是外觀如此。在內部，牆上滿是巨大的畫作，展示華格納歌劇和德國傳說的場景。螺旋狀的樓梯消失在高塔裡，黃金枝形吊燈懸掛在天花板上，而光是路德維希寢室裡的木頭就由 14 個人花了將近五年才雕刻完成。

❹ 打造夢想可不便宜。到了 1885 年，在各式各樣的宮殿和城堡花掉他所有的錢之後，路德維希負債 1,400 萬馬克。但新天鵝堡尚未完工，路德維希想借更多的錢。路德維希國王的大臣決定，他們必須阻止他。四位醫生簽署了一份報告，宣告國王精神錯亂。「你們怎麼能宣告我精神錯亂？」路德維希抱怨說。「畢竟，你們從來沒看過或檢查過我！」抗議歸抗議，路德維希還

是被奪了權。過不到一星期，他就被人發現漂浮在湖面，死了。湖水很淺，而且路德維希國王據說很會游泳。他的死因至今依舊成謎。

❺ 1886 年，路德維希辭世七週後，新天鵝堡對遊客開放了。政府的財政大臣需要籌措一些錢。此後幾年，新天鵝堡成了歐洲最著名的建築之一。數以百萬的遊客去德國參觀這座完美的童話城堡，一如好的童話該具備的一樣，它本身也有不可告人的祕密。長年下來，路德維希的新天鵝堡所賺的錢已足夠讓它一次又一次回本了。

 **精要句型**

■ **Neuschwanstein *is nothing if not* dramatic.**
新天鵝堡十分具有戲劇性。

句型 **X is nothing if not Y.**「X 十分 Y。」

這個句型是以更有趣（與更強烈）的方式來表達：X is definitely Y!

例句 Professor Chen *is nothing if not* ambitious.
陳教授十分有企圖心。

She'*s nothing if not* serious.
她十分認真。

詞彙測驗

Match the words from the box to the speakers.

debt	fantasy	shallow	fairy tale	composer	tribute

_____ **1.** We can swim here, but don't dive. The water isn't deep enough.

_____ **2.** Nobody understands my new opera. Fools!

_____ **3.** In order to express our gratitude, respect and admiration, we are building a giant snowman that looks just like our teacher, Mr. Palmer.

_____ **4.** Sometimes, instead of doing my homework, I imagine that I am a vampire, and I think about whose blood I would drink.

5. "Once upon a time in the middle of winter, when the flakes of snow were falling like feathers from the sky, a queen sat at a window sewing ..."

6. You owed me thirty dollars before I owed you forty, so now I owe you ten, right?

旅 遊 一 點 通

去參觀新天鵝堡時，舊天鵝堡的慕勒飯店可能是最理想的住宿地點。訂間套房，當你在戶外的陽台上放鬆時，就能看到城堡。花 35 分鐘，就可以從飯店走到城堡。路德維希幼時所住的舊天鵝堡，則只要走五分鐘就到了。在春天（一片翠綠、花朵盛開）、秋天（所有的樹葉都會改變顏色）和冬天（一片白雪）時，風景都很漂亮。可到下列網站查看慕勒飯店與訂房：

http://www.hotel-mueller.de/45.html

旅遊好用句
在開始走之前，要先確定自己走對了路：
Is this the trail to Neuschwanstein?
「這是通往新天鵝堡的路嗎？」

解 答

 詞彙測驗

把框框裡的字彙跟說話者配對。

1. shallow

譯文 我們可以在這裡游泳，但不要跳水。水不夠深。

2. composer

譯文 沒有人懂我的新歌劇。笨蛋！

3. tribute

譯文 為了表示我們的感謝、尊敬與推崇，我們做了一個巨大的雪人，而且長得就像我們的老師帕默先生。

4. fantasy

譯文 有時候我會放下功課，想像自己是個吸血鬼，並思索著要去吸誰的血。

5. fairy tale

譯文 「在很久以前的一個寒冬，雪花片片落下，就像羽毛飄在空中，有一位皇后坐在窗邊刺繡……」

6. debt

譯文 在我欠你 40 塊之前，你欠了我 30 塊，所以現在我欠你 10 塊，對吧？

UNIT 16 | Stonehenge
圓形石林

Located in United Kingdom（英國）

1 In a grassy¹ field in England, some big rocks are arranged in circles. That's Stonehenge. It doesn't sound like much, does it? Disappointed visitors have been known to conclude that it doesn't *look* like much, either. Why is Stonehenge world-famous? What's the big deal?

2 The short answer is this: Stonehenge is mysterious.² Nobody knows for certain why Stonehenge was built or how it was used. Thousands of years after it was constructed, Stonehenge still fascinates³ and inspires us at least partly because we do not fully understand it.

3 Stonehenge was built in phases.⁴ First, around 3000 BC, somebody made a henge⁵—a circular ditch⁶ and bank⁷ of earth. Many archaeologists⁸ believe this original henge was a sacred place for burying the dead. Building henges used to be a popular activity in the region. Thousands remain, all around Britain. Stonehenge is the most famous. The stones standing inside the henge were added between 2600 BC and 2200 BC.

Ⓦⓞⓡⓓ Ⓛⓘⓢⓣ ─────────────────

1. grassy〔`græsɪ〕*adj.* 多草的；草深的
2. mysterious〔mɪs`tɪrɪəs〕*adj.* 神秘的
3. fascinate〔`fæsṇ‚et〕*v.* 使……著迷
4. phase〔fez〕*n.* 階段；時期
5. henge〔hɛndʒ〕*n.* 石陣
6. ditch〔dɪtʃ〕*n.* 壕溝；水溝
7. bank〔bæŋk〕*n.* 土堤；堤防

At the very center of Stonehenge, enormous[9] stones weighing thousands of kilograms each are set up together to look like giant doorways: two stones stand vertically with a third stone placed across the top. They're called trilithons.[10] Their simple, elemental design achieves a majestic,[11] moving effect.

❹ Ringed[12] around the trilithons are a number of bluestones (they look blue when wet), which apparently came from mountains in Wales, 250 kilometers away. Why would anybody take the trouble to move these huge stones so far? One theory: the prehistoric[13] people who built Stonehenge believed the bluestones to have magical healing powers. Human teeth and bones showing evidence of various injuries and illnesses have been dug up at Stonehenge. Some archaeologists believe these are the remains[14] of people who traveled to Stonehenge to be healed.

❺ In the past, people found it difficult to believe that normal men had

---

8. archaeologist 〔͵ɑrkɪˋɑlədʒɪst〕 *n.* 考古學家
9. enormous 〔ɪˋnɔrməs〕 *adj.* 巨大的；龐大的
10. trilithon 〔traɪˋlɪθɑn〕 *n.* 三石塔
11. majestic 〔məˋdʒɛstɪk〕 *adj.* 莊嚴的；堂皇的
12. ring 〔rɪŋ〕 *v.* 圍繞；包圍
13. prehistoric 〔͵prihɪsˋtɔrɪk〕 *adj.* 史前的；先史時代的
14. remains 〔rɪˋmenz〕 *n.* (*pl.*) 遺骸

actually moved the stones. According to one popular legend, a wizard[15] named Merlin brought them using magic. Some people suspected the Devil was involved. Others, more recently, have said that moving the stones would have been an *easy* job—for aliens[16] from outer space. In reality, a large number of incredibly[17] determined, hardworking but otherwise normal men must have used simple tools and lots of muscle power to push, drag, and roll the stones into place. After coming all the way from Wales with the rocks, those guys were *definitely* in need of some healing.

❻ Some of the theories about Stonehenge do make a lot more sense than others. So far, though, nobody has come up with a complete explanation. Maybe that's fine. Too much explanation sometimes makes things seem small and disappointing. Often we are inspired most by those things we do not completely understand.

15. wizard 〔`wɪzəd〕 *n.* 巫師
16. alien 〔`elɪən〕 *n.* 外星人
17. incredibly 〔ɪn`krɛdəblɪ〕 *adv.* 難以置信地;驚人地

譯文

❶ 在英格蘭的一片草原上，有一些大石頭被排成圓形，那就是圓形石林。它聽起來沒什麼，對吧？據說失望的遊客認定，它「看起來」也沒什麼。圓形石林為什麼會舉世聞名？它厲害在哪裡？

❷ 簡短的回答如下：圓形石林很「神秘」。沒有人確實知道，圓形石林為什麼要建造，或者有什麼用。蓋好幾千年後，圓形石林仍然吸引並啓發著我們，部分原因就是因為我們不完全了解它。

❸ 圓形石林是分階段建造。首先，在西元前 3000 年左右，有人做了個石陣，也就是圓形的渠道與土堤。許多考古學家相信，這個最初的石陣是埋葬死者的聖地。建造石陣在當地是很普遍的作法。留下來的有成千上萬座，遍布在英國各地。最有名的就是圓形石林。石陣內所樹立的石頭是在西元前 2600 年到西元前 2200 年之間所增加。在圓形石林的正中央，一塊塊重達幾千公斤的巨石被擺在一起，看起來就像個巨大的出入口：兩塊石頭垂直站立，第三塊石頭則橫架在頂上。它們被稱為三石塔。它們簡單的基本設計展現了壯觀且動人的效果。

❹ 環繞在三石塔周圍的是一些青石（它們濕的時候看起來是藍色的），而且顯然是取自遠在 250 公里外的威爾斯山區。為什麼有人要大費周章地把這些巨石搬這麼遠？有一個理論是：建造圓形石林的史前人類相信，青石有神奇的治療力量。在圓形石林裡曾挖出人類的牙齒與骨頭，可以看出不同傷口與疾病的證據。有些考古學家相信，這些遺骸是屬於前往圓形石林接受治療的人。

❺ 過去，人們很難相信石頭真的是由平凡人所搬動。根據一則普遍的傳說，

有個叫做梅林的巫師用魔法把它們弄了過來。有些人則懷疑是魔鬼動的手腳。到了比較近期，有些人覺得對來自外太空的外星人而言，搬動石頭是「輕而易舉」的事。實際上，那一定是靠許許多多擁有無比決心、努力工作的平凡人，利用簡單的工具和大量的肌力把石頭推、拉、滾到定位。在把岩石從威爾斯一路帶來後，那些人「肯定」需要一些治療了。

6 關於圓形石林的某些理論的確比其他理論來得有道理。不過到目前為止，沒有人提出過完整的解釋。也許這樣也無妨，有時候過多的解釋會讓事情顯得渺小與令人失望。對我們啟發最大的往往都是那些我們不完全了解的東西。

🗝️ 精要句型

■ **Stonehenge** *doesn't sound like much*.
圓形石林聽起來沒什麼。

句型 **X doesn't sound like much.** 「X 聽起來沒什麼。」

這句慣用語還有下列類似用法：

X doesn't look like much. 「X 看起來沒什麼。」

X doesn't look/sound/seem like much of a Y. 「X 看起來 / 聽起來 / 似乎不太像 Y。」

例句 He's short and he *doesn't look like much of* a basketball player, but wait until you see him play.
他很矮，看起來不太像個籃球員，但等你看到他打球再說吧。

I saw Fiona's new house. It *doesn't look like much*, but it's in a good neighborhood.
我看到了費歐娜的新房子。它看起來沒什麼，但附近的環境不錯。

✏️ 詞彙測驗

Look at the words that go together with "legend" and use them to complete the sentences.

local		living
	legend	
according to		become

1. American folksinger Bob Dylan is a _____ legend. Is he also a good singer?

2. _____ legend, Robin Hood stole from the rich and gave to the poor.

3. Hannah knows she wants to _____ a legend—she just isn't quite sure how to get started.

4. Freshman Timmy Munson became a _____ legend in Middletown after he scored 10 points in 5 seconds to help the Wolves win the City Basketball Championship.

旅 遊 一 點 通

在圓形石林，遊客通常不可以觸摸或者太靠近石頭。假如你安排私人的團體參訪（電話：+44 (0) 1722 34 38 34），就可以靠近一點，而且會很值得：近看石頭會讓你留下深刻印象。每年在夏至期間（6月20日到21日），圓形石林會舉行慶典，並允許民眾走入石陣中。參閱下列網站可以了解相關資訊：

http://www.english-heritage.org.uk/server/show/nav.16465

旅遊好用句

如果要預約團體參訪，最好提前以電話聯絡：

Hello. I'm calling to arrange a group visit to Stonehenge. Do you have any openings during the third week of February?

「你好，我打電話來是要安排團體參訪圓形石林。你們在二月的第三週有任何名額嗎？」

詞彙測驗

請看看跟「legend」搭配使用的字彙，並用它們來完成句子。

1. living

譯文 美國民歌手巴布‧狄倫是個活傳奇。他也是個好歌手嗎？

2. According to

譯文 根據傳說，羅賓漢會劫富濟貧。

3. become

譯文 漢娜知道自己想成為傳奇——她只是不太確定要怎麼起步才好。

4. local

譯文 大一新鮮人提米‧孟森成了米德爾敦的當地傳奇，因為他在五秒內得了十分，並協助狼隊贏得了城市盃籃球錦標賽。

PART 4

北美洲

UNIT 17 | Chichén Itzá
奇琴伊察

Located in Mexico（墨西哥）

❶ In the movie *The Ruins*, a group of young tourists hike through the jungle in Mexico to visit an ancient Mayan[1] pyramid that looks a lot like the one at Chichén Itzá. Only the movie pyramid is covered with a dark green people-eating vampire vine.[2] And it's hungry—very hungry. You might not want to watch that movie right before you go to Mexico.

❷ The real pyramid is safe from vampire vines. It's called *El Castillo*—Spanish for "The Castle." Rising up dramatically in the center of the site known as Chichén Itzá, on the Yucatan Peninsula in southern Mexico, it was built 800 to 1,000 years ago by the Mayans. The temple on top of *El Castillo* is dedicated to the Mayan god Kukulkan, who takes the form of a feathered[3] serpent.[4]

❸ The Mayans were good astronomers.[5] *El Castillo* was designed with mathematical precision[6] to interact with the sun, kind of like a fancy, three-dimensional[7] calendar. On two special days each year (the spring and autumn equinoxes)[8] the sun shines past the corners of the pyramid's step-like layers and casts[9] a shadow upon the slanting[10] railing[11] of the north stairs. The shadow looks like a giant serpent, emerging from the top of the pyramid. As the sun moves through the

---

Ⓦⓞⓡⓓ Ⓛⓘⓢⓣ ————————————————

1. Mayan〔`majən〕 *adj.* 馬雅族的　*n.* 馬雅人
2. vine〔vaɪn〕 *n.* 藤；蔓
3. feather〔`fɛðɚ〕 *v.* 飾以羽毛
4. serpent〔`sɝpənt〕 *n.* 蛇
5. astronomer〔ə`strɑnəmɚ〕 *n.* 天文學家
6. precision〔prɪ`sɪʒən〕 *n.* 精密；精確
7. dimensional〔də`mɛnʃənḷ〕 *adj.* (……度) 空間的

sky, the shadow-serpent crawls down the side of the pyramid until it merges with the head of Kukulkan, sculpted[12] in stone at the base of the stairs. Then it retreats[13] back up the pyramid, disappearing for another six months.

❹ Besides worshipping serpent gods, the Mayans also liked sports. Not far from *El Castillo* is another one of Chichén Itzá's famous buildings: the Great Ball Court. Open to the sky, the court is 166 meters long and 68 meters wide, with 12-meter stone walls on each side. Mounted[14] high on the walls are stone rings carved like serpents, which may have been

8. equinox〔`ikwə,nɑks〕*n.* 春（秋）分；晝夜平分時
9. cast〔kæst〕*v.* 拋；擲
10. slant〔slænt〕*v.* 使……歪斜；使……傾斜
11. railing〔`relɪŋ〕*n.* 扶欄；柵欄
12. sculpt〔skʌlpt〕*v.* 雕刻
13. retreat〔rɪ`trit〕*v.* 後退；撤退
14. mount〔maʊnt〕*v.* 登上；安裝

used as goals.

❺ The exact rules of the game are unknown. Historians[15] believe it was played with a solid rubber ball that weighed as much as four kilograms. Players knocked the heavy ball back and forth[16] with their hips.[17] The Spaniard Diego Durán, who saw a later version of the game, wrote that players received terrible bruises and were sometimes even killed if the ball hit them wrong.

❻ The stone walls of the court are carved with images of ball players. One of the players, perhaps one of the losers, has had his head cut off. Blood spurts[18] from his neck in seven streams, six of which turn into serpents. The seventh spurting stream of blood becomes a twisting, snake-like vine—kind of like the vampire vine in that movie. Don't think about it too much.

15. historian〔hɪsˋtorɪən〕 *n.* 歷史學家
16. back and forth *adv.* 來回地
17. hip〔hɪp〕 *n.* 臀部（連接腿和軀幹的突起部分）
18. spurt〔spɜt〕 *v.* 噴出

譯文

❶ 在電影《禁入廢墟》裡，有一群年輕遊客徒步穿越墨西哥的叢林，去參觀古老的馬雅金字塔。它看起來跟奇琴伊察的那座頗為相像，只不過電影裡的金字塔上爬滿了深綠色會吃人的吸血藤，而且它很餓——餓極了。在你要去墨西哥的前夕，你可能不會想看那部電影的。

❷ 真的金字塔不會受到吸血藤危害。它叫做「卡斯提歐」，在西班牙文裡是「城堡」的意思。昂然聳立在被稱為奇琴伊察的遺址中央，地點在墨西哥南部的猶加敦半島，它是在 800 到 1,000 年前由馬雅人所建造。卡斯提歐頂上的寺廟是在供奉馬雅神祇庫庫爾坎，祂是以羽蛇的形態出現。

❸ 馬雅人是很棒的天文學家。卡斯提歐是用精確的數學設計成能跟太陽互動，有點像一座豪華的三度空間曆法。在每年兩個特別的日子裡（春分和秋分），陽光會照到金字塔階梯式層級的角落，並使陰影籠罩在北邊階梯的傾斜欄杆上。這片陰影看起來就像一條大蛇，從金字塔的頂端冒出來。隨著太陽劃過天際，陰影蛇會沿著金字塔的邊往下爬，直到跟庫庫爾坎的頭合為一體為止。庫庫爾坎的頭刻在階梯底部的石頭上。接著影子會退回到金字塔的上方，消失六個月。

❹ 除了崇拜蛇神外，馬雅人還喜歡運動。在卡斯提歐的不遠處，有奇琴伊察的另一座著名建築：大球場。這座露天場地長 166 公尺，寬 68 公尺，每一面都有 12 公尺高的石牆。牆上的高處裝設了刻得像蛇的石環，可能是用來當作目標。

❺ 比賽的確切規則不得而知。歷史家相信，它打的是實心的橡皮球，重達四公斤之多，選手用臀部把重球來回頂來頂去。西班牙人迪亞哥·杜蘭看過後

來的比賽版本，他寫道，選手嚴重瘀傷，而且假如球沒打好，有時候甚至還會送命。

❻ 場地的石牆上刻有球賽選手的圖案。其中有個選手大概是打輸了，所以遭到斬首。他的脖子噴出了七道血，其中六道變成了蛇。第七道噴出來的血則化成了交纏的蛇狀藤，有點像是那部電影裡的吸血藤。可別太常想著它了。

🔑 精要句型

■ **And it's** *hungry—very hungry.*

而且它很餓——餓極了。

句型 **Somebody/something is X—very X.** 「某人／某事……——……極

了。」

這個句型用來強調 X 這個特質，並讓讀者思考 X 到底是什麼狀況。

例句 A: What's summer like in Kaohsiung? B: It's *hot—very hot.*

A：高雄的夏天是什麼樣子？ B：很熱——熱極了。

Mom knows we ate the cake. She's *mad—very, very mad.*

老媽知道我們把蛋糕吃了。她很氣——氣極了。

📝 詞彙測驗

(   ) **1.** The word **base** in paragraph 3, line 12 is closest in meaning to

      A. opening   B. most

      C. bottom   D. first

(   ) **2.** The word **mounted** in paragraph 4, line 9 is closest in meaning to

      A. attached   B. climbed

      C. thrown   D. hidden

(   ) **3.** The words **emerging from** in paragraph 3, line 7 are closest in

     meaning to

      A. disappearing into   B. giving to

      C. depending upon   D. coming out of

4. Look in the essay to find the opposites of these words.

1) inexactness   _____

2) advance   _____

3) minor   _____

4) unimpressively   _____

5) earlier   _____

旅 遊 一 點 通

去墨西哥前，一定要弄本卡爾‧法蘭茲（Carl Franz）的書《庶民的墨西哥指南》（*The People's Guide to Mexico: Wherever You Go, There You Are!!*）來看。法蘭茲並不是著重於哪些飯店最便宜，或者哪些夜店最受歡迎。相反地，他是在教你要怎麼了解和欣賞墨西哥，要怎麼自力更生，以及要怎麼隨遇而安。要小心的是，在看完書後，你可能會取消所有原訂計畫，並立刻動身去尋求冒險。可以上這個網站多了解一下：

http://www.peoplesguide.com/

旅遊好用句

如果你的同伴對每個小問題都抱怨連連，那就對他說：

Look, wherever you go, there you are! So let's try to make the best of it, OK?

「聽好，不管你去哪裡，你人就在那裡了！所以我們盡量樂在其中，好嗎？」

詞彙測驗

1. 第三段第十二行中的「base」這個字最接近的意義是

A. 開口　B. 最　C. 底部　D. 最初

Ans　C

2. 第四段第九行中的「mounted」這個字最接近的意義是

A. 裝　B. 爬　C. 丟　D. 藏

Ans　A

3. 第三段第七行中的「emerging from」這個詞最接近的意義是

A. 消失於　B. 給　C. 依靠　D. 出現

Ans　D

4. 從文中找出這些單字的反義字。

1) precision 精確

2) retreat 退

3) terrible 嚴重的

4) dramatically 戲劇化地

5) later 後來

UNIT
18 | The Statue of Liberty
自由女神像

Located in the United States（美國）

❶ In 1886, France gave the United States a big present. It was a gesture of friendship, meant to celebrate America's 100th birthday (actually, the present arrived 10 years late) and to honor the ideals shared by the two countries. The present arrived in pieces, in 210 boxes, on a ship. When the pieces were put together on a small island in New York Harbor, they became the Statue¹ of Liberty.

❷ The Statue of Liberty is a giant copper² woman, dressed in robes. She is 46 meters tall and has a lovely 1.5 meter nose. Created by the sculptor Frédéric Auguste Bartholdi in a Paris workshop, the statue's face was rumored³ to be based on Bartholdi's mother, while the body was said to be modeled after his girlfriend. Another Frenchman, Gustave Eiffel (see Unit 14), engineered the complex internal structure of the statue.

❸ To raise money for the podium⁴ upon which the statue would stand, a New York newspaper asked for contributions. Many

---

Ⓦ Ⓞ Ⓡ Ⓓ Ⓛ Ⓘ Ⓢ Ⓣ

1. statue〔ˋstætʃʊ〕 *n.* 雕像
2. copper〔ˋkɑpɚ〕 *n.* 銅
3. rumor〔ˋrumɚ〕 *v.* 謠傳
4. podium〔ˋpodɪəm〕 *n.* 作為基座的高石台
5. circus〔ˋsɝkəs〕 *n.* 馬戲團；馬戲表演
6. torch〔tɔrtʃ〕 *n.* 火炬；火把

regular Americans sent money. "We have taken three lessons in French and we don't like it," said one letter, "but we love the good French people for giving us the beautiful statue, and we send you a dollar—the money we had saved to go to the circus." [5]

❹ In her right hand, Liberty holds up a torch[6] that represents enlightenment.[7] The broken chains under her feet symbolize freedom from oppression.[8] In her left hand, she holds a tablet[9] (no, it's not an Apple iPad) upon which is written the date of the American Declaration of Independence: July 4, 1776. The most famous sentence from the Declaration of Independence says that all men are created equal and that everybody has the same basic right to life, liberty, and the pursuit of happiness.

❺ When moviemakers[10] want to show that the United States is in trouble, they show the Statue of Liberty buried or frozen or broken or getting her head chopped off.[11] When their country fails to live up to[12] its

---

7. enlightenment〔ɪn`laɪtŋmənt〕*n.* 教化；啓發
8. oppression〔ə`prɛʃən〕*n.* 壓迫；壓抑
9. tablet〔`tæblɪt〕*n.* 碑；牌；匾額
10. moviemaker〔`muvɪˌmekə〕*n.* 電影製片者
11. chop off 砍下
12. live up to 符合（期望等）

ideals, Americans imagine the Statue crying, or bent over holding her head in shame.

❻ Americans have also used the Statue of Liberty to stress the importance of other values. Instead of the torch of enlightenment, for example, the Statue was once shown holding up a donut. Another time, Lady Liberty's exposed right underarm[13] was used in a commercial for deodorant.[14]

❼ The Statue of Liberty has perhaps been most meaningful to America's immigrants.[15] The United States accepts more immigrants than any other country in the world. Many used to arrive by boat. The first thing they saw in America was

the Statue of Liberty. Even after learning about America's imperfections,[16] many still remember it as one of the happiest moments of their lives.

Ⓦ Ⓞ Ⓡ Ⓓ Ⓛ Ⓘ Ⓢ Ⓣ

13. underarm〔ˋʌndəͺɑrm〕 *n.* 腋下
14. deodorant〔diˋodərənt〕 *n.* 止汗劑；防臭劑
15. immigrant〔ˋɪməgrənt〕 *n.* (來自外國的) 移民
16. imperfection〔ͺɪmpəˋfɛkʃən〕 *n.* 不完善；不完美

譯文

❶ 1886 年時，法國送了一份大禮給美國。它代表著友誼，以藉此祝賀美國的 100 歲生日（實際上，這份賀禮晚了 10 年才送達），並表彰兩國共同的理想。這份禮物是用船一塊塊運來的，裝在 210 個箱子裡。當每一塊在紐約港的小島上組合起來時，它就成了自由女神像。

❷ 自由女神像是個銅製的女巨人，身著長袍。她有 46 公尺高，還有 1.5 公尺的漂亮鼻子。它是由雕刻家斐德烈克‧奧古斯特‧巴托爾迪在巴黎的工坊所建造，這座雕像的長相據傳是取自巴托爾迪的母親，身體據說是以他的女友為範本。另一位法國人古斯塔夫‧艾菲爾（參見第 14 章）則為雕像打造了複雜的內部結構。

❸ 為了替放置雕像的基座籌措經費，紐約一家報紙發起了捐款。許多美國百姓都捐了錢。「我們上過三堂法文課，我們不喜歡它。」有一封信寫道。「可是我們樂見法國的好人送我們美麗的雕像，所以我們捐一元給你們──這筆錢我們本來是要存來看馬戲團的。」

❹ 在她的右手上，自由女神握著一支代表啓蒙的火炬。她腳下所踩的斷鏈則是象徵免於壓迫的自由。在她的左手上，她拿著一塊書簡（不，那不是蘋果的 iPad），上面記載著美國宣布獨立的日期：1776 年 7 月 4 日（註：日期是以羅馬數字呈現）。獨立宣言中最有名的句子說道：人人生而平等，每個人都有生存、自由與追求幸福的相同基本權利。

❺ 當拍電影的人想要表現出美國遇到麻煩時，他們就會讓自由女神像被掩埋、冰凍、擊毀，或者頭被砍掉。當國家無法實現理想時，美國人就會想像神像在哭泣，或是羞愧地彎腰抱頭。

❻ 美國人也會用自由女神像來強調其他價值的重要性。例如神像曾經被設計成握著甜甜圈，而不是啓蒙的火炬。還有一次，女神外露的右手腋下則被運用在除臭劑的電視廣告中。

❼ 自由女神像對於美國的外來移民大概是最有意義的。美國比世界上其他任何一個國家接受了更多的移民。很多人以往都是乘船而來，而他們在美國看到的第一樣東西就是自由女神像。即使在了解到美國的不完美後，很多人依然記得，那是生命中最幸福的時刻之一。

精要句型

■ *Even after* learning about America's imperfections, many immigrants *still* remember their first sight of the Statue of Liberty as one of the happiest moments of their lives.

即使在了解到美國的不完美後，很多人依然記得，第一次看到自由女神像是生命中最幸福的時刻之一。

句型 **Even after X, ... still Y.**「即使經過 X，仍然 Y。」

可用來表示，Y 在某方面相當穩固，足以抵擋 X 的影響。

例句 *Even after* her mother threatened to send her to bed early, Jasmine *still* refused to eat the carrots.

即使在母親威脅要早早把她送上床後，潔斯敏依然拒絕吃胡蘿蔔。

Andrew *still* wanted to go fishing, *even after* the weatherman said a typhoon was coming.

安德魯依然想要去釣魚，即使在氣象預報員說有颱風要來後。

詞彙測驗

Match the words from the box to the speakers.

liberty	immigrants	sculptor	frozen	meaningful

_____ **1.** Is this exercise important? Yes, it is. Right now, it's the most important thing in my life. I care about it with all my heart, and I am determined to get it right.

2. It's too cold. If we can't get a fire started, we're going to die. I hear it's not a bad way to go—kind of like falling asleep.

3. Look—I'm a reasonable person, a nice person. As long as I don't hurt anyone, I want to be free to make my own decisions. I don't like to get bossed around. It makes me mean.

4. His new project really surprised me. It's a stainless steel squid, five meters tall.

5. "America has constantly drawn strength and spirit from them. They have proved to be the most restless, the most adventurous, the most innovative, the most industrious of people." [said President Bill Clinton.]

旅 遊 一 點 通

通往自由女神像火炬的階梯從 1916 年起就已對外關閉。在正常情況下，可以往上爬到神像的皇冠那麼遠，那裡有窗戶可以看到水面和紐約市（神像面對著布魯克林）。但在 2001 年 9 月 11 日，紐約市遭到恐怖攻擊後，自由女神像就關閉了好幾年。如今它重新開放，但遊客可能不准爬到基座以上的地方。可以上神像的官方網站去查詢現況：

http://www.nps.gov/stli/index.htm

旅遊好用句

可以事先打電話去問問，神像有哪些地方對外開放：

I'll be visiting the Statue of Liberty in July. Will the crown be open to the public then?

「我 7 月要去參觀自由女神像。到時候皇冠會對外開放嗎？」

解 答

詞彙測驗

把框框裡的單字跟說話者配對。

1. meaningful

譯文 這個練習重要嗎？是的，重要。目前它是我生命中最重要的事。我十分在乎，而且我下定決心要把它做好。

2. frozen

譯文 天氣太冷了。假如我們沒辦法生火，我們就死定了。聽說那樣的死法還不賴，有點像是睡著了。

3. liberty

譯文 聽著，我是個講理的人，也是個好人。只要我不會傷害到任何人，我就希望照自己的意思自由決定。我不喜歡被呼來喚去，那會讓我很不舒服。

4. sculptor

譯文 他的新案子讓我大感意外。那是個不鏽鋼烏賊，有五公尺高。

5. immigrants

譯文 「美國不斷從他們身上獲取力量與精神。他們證明了自己是最不眠不休、最勇於冒險、最創新、最勤奮的人。」〔比爾·柯林頓總統說。〕

PART 5

南美洲

UNIT 19 | **Machu Picchu**
馬丘比丘

Located in Peru（秘魯）

❶ It looks like a place where a dragon would build its nest. Sharp mountain peaks stick up all around. Dense[1] green jungle grows everywhere. Wet clouds float close by. And there, on a steep, narrow ridge,[2] high in the Andes Mountains, is a startling[3] sight: a city made of stone. It is called Machu Picchu, and it is one of the world's great lost cities. Machu Picchu was built by the Incas[4] in the 15th century. When the Spanish conquered the Inca Empire in the 16th century, they looted[5] every Inca site they could find for gold and other treasures. They never found Machu Picchu. The mountains and the jungle hid it too well.

❷ The city was abandoned[6] and lost to the outside world until 1911, when an explorer[7] named Hiram Bingham went to Peru and climbed 450 meters up a ridge above the Urubamba River. A local farmer had told him there were old stone buildings up there. What Bingham found took his breath away.

❸ There are about 200 buildings at Machu Picchu, with space for more than 1,000 people. There are homes and temples and

Ⓦ Ⓞ Ⓡ Ⓓ Ⓛ Ⓘ Ⓢ Ⓣ

1. dense 〔dɛns〕 *adj.* 密集的
2. ridge 〔rɪdʒ〕 *n.* 山背；山脊
3. startling 〔ˋstɑrtl̩ɪŋ〕 *adj.* 驚人的；使人吃驚的
4. Inca 〔ˋɪŋkə〕 *n.* 印加族
5. loot 〔lut〕 *v.* 掠奪；侵佔
6. abandon 〔əˋbændən〕 *v.* 遺棄；拋棄
7. explorer 〔ɪkˋsplorə〕 *n.* 探險家

fountains. There are terraces[8] that look like staircases[9] made for giants. At a high point in the city, there is a piano-sized rock carved and positioned so that it works as an astrological[10] clock.

❹ The roofs of the buildings are gone, but the walls remain. Inca walls are beautiful. They are made with big, heavy stones. Every stone is a different size and shape. The Incas fit the irregular[11] stones together like the pieces of a puzzle.[12]

❺ Machu Picchu was built by the Inca Emperor of the time, Pachacuti. Many archaeologists[13] believe it was a home away from home for him and other members of the Inca royal family. Machu Picchu is about five days by foot from Cuzco, the Inca capital city where Pachacuti normally lived.

8. terrace〔`tɛrɪs〕 *n.* 梯台
9. staircase〔`stɛrˌkes〕 *n.* 樓梯
10. astrological〔ˌæstrə`lɑdʒɪkl̩〕 *adj.* 占星的
11. irregular〔ɪ`rɛgjələ〕 *adj.* 不規則的
12. puzzle〔`pʌzl̩〕 *n.* 拼圖；字謎
13. archaeologist〔ˌɑrkɪ`ɑlədʒɪst〕 *n.* 考古學家

❻ In Quechua—the language of the Incas which is still spoken by many people in Peru today—Machu Picchu means "Old Peak." All the mountains around Machu Picchu have names. The jagged[14] rock that rises directly above Machu Picchu is called Huayna Picchu—"Young Peak." The Incas worshipped the high, snowy mountains of the Andes[15] as gods.

❼ An Inca Emperor had lots of privileges.[16] Pachacuti's followers saw him as a god. Virgin girls caught his spit before it touched the ground. He wore magnificent[17] clothes made from the finest vicuña[18] wool, never the same outfit twice. All that must have been great fun, but Pachacuti's greatest perk[19] may have been to be surrounded by the mountains and the clouds and the sky, while hanging out as the guest of honor at Machu Picchu.

Ⓦ Ⓞ Ⓡ Ⓓ Ⓛ Ⓘ Ⓢ Ⓣ

14. jagged〔ˋdʒægɪd〕 *adj.* 鋸齒狀的；有缺口的
15. Andes〔ˋændɪz〕 *n.* 安地斯山脈
16. privilege〔ˋprɪvlɪdʒ〕 *n.* 特權
17. magnificent〔mægˋnɪfəsṇt〕 *adj.* 宏偉的；壯麗的
18. vicuña〔vɪˋkjunə〕 *n.* 駱馬
19. perk〔pɝk〕 *n.* 額外補貼

譯文

❶ 它看起來就像個龍會去築巢的地方。尖尖的山峰在四面八方挺立，濃密的翠綠叢林到處生長，還有濕雲飄浮在側。在安地斯山脈高處一個又陡又窄的山脊上，那裡有個令人歎為觀止的景象：一座用石頭打造出來的城市。它叫做馬丘比丘，是世界上最大的失落城市之一。馬丘比丘是由印加人在 15 世紀所建造。西班牙人在 16 世紀征服印加帝國後，洗劫了每個能找到黃金和其他寶物的印加據點。但他們從來沒發現馬丘比丘。山脈和叢林把它藏得太好了。

❷ 在 1911 年之前，這座城市一直被外界棄置與遺忘，此時有一位叫做海勒姆‧賓厄姆的探險家到秘魯，爬了 450 公尺高來到烏魯班巴河上方的山脊。當地有一位農民告訴他，那上面有古老的石造建築。賓厄姆所發現的東西令他屏息。

❸ 馬丘比丘大約有 200 座建築，可容納 1,000 人以上。其中有住家、寺廟和噴泉。有的梯台看起來像是替巨人建造的樓梯。在城市的高點，有塊鋼琴大小的岩石經過了雕刻與定位，以當作天文鐘。

❹ 建築的屋頂不見了，但牆面仍在。印加的牆面很漂亮。它們是用又大又重的石頭所砌成，而且每塊石頭的大小和形狀都不一樣。印加人把不規則的石頭組合起來，宛如一塊塊的拼圖。

❺ 馬丘比丘是由當時的印加皇帝帕查庫提所興建。許多考古學家相信，這是他和印加皇室其他成員的別館。帕查庫提通常是住在印加的首都庫斯科，而從那裡走路去馬丘比丘則要五天左右。

❻ 在克丘亞語中——時至今日，秘魯仍有許多人在說這種印加語——馬丘比丘是「古峰」的意思。馬丘比丘周圍的山脈全都有名字。聳立在馬丘比丘正上方的鋸齒狀岩石被稱為瓦伊納比丘——也就是「幼峰」。印加人把高聳多雪的安地斯山脈奉為神明。

❼ 印加皇帝擁有許多特權。帕查庫提的信徒視他為神明。年輕的處女會在他的痰碰到地上前把它接住。他所穿的華服是用最上等的比庫尼亞毛所織成，而且同一套衣服從來不穿兩次。這一切一定頗有樂趣，但帕查庫提最大的福利或許是被群山、雲朵和天空所包圍，以及遊蕩在馬丘比丘當個貴客。

 精要句型

■ **Machu Picchu *is about five days by foot from* Cuzco.**
從庫斯科走路去馬丘比丘要五天左右。

句型 **Place¹ is + time + by foot from place².** 「從地方 1 到地方 2 步行
要……（時間）。」

By foot 也可替換成其他交通方式，如：by plane「搭飛機」、by train
「坐火車」、by bus「搭公車」等。

例句 The MRT station *is 20 minutes by foot from* here.
從這邊到捷運站走路要 20 分鐘左右。

Taichung *is just 2 hours by bus from* Taipei.
從台北到台中搭公車只要二小時。

詞彙測驗

1. Look in the essay to find the opposites of these words.

a) regular   _____

b) whole   _____

c) dropped   _____

d) always   _____

e) didn't surprise him at all   _____

(   ) **2.** The word **royal** in paragraph 5, line 3 is closest in meaning to

A. important

B. leading

C. noble

D. king

( ) **3.** The word **privileges** in paragraph 7, line 2 is closest in meaning to

    A. benefits

    B. treasures

    C. laws

    D. gifts

( ) **4.** The word **conquered** in paragraph 1, line 7 is closest in meaning to

    A. travel around

    B. take over

    C. join with

    D. come from

旅 遊 一 點 通

秘魯料理不如法式或中式料理有名，但它有這樣的實力。秘魯好吃到令人上癮的國菜叫做 ceviche。它是用鮮魚來製作，魚是吃生的，事先會用酸橙汁醃過，並配上切片洋蔥、辣椒和一、兩樣獨門香料。裡面經常會加蝦子和章魚。Ceviche 是搭配白飯、烤玉米和幾片番薯來吃。趁魚還很新鮮的時候，點它來當作早午餐。Ceviche 非常棒，光是爲了它，就值得跑一趟秘魯了。

旅遊好用句

假如你點的海鮮看起來不太新鮮，爲了安全起見，可以跟服務生反應：

I'm sorry. The seafood doesn't seem too fresh. I'd like to order something different.

「抱歉，海鮮似乎不太新鮮。我想點別的。」

解 答

 詞彙測驗

1. 從文章中找出這些字彙的反義字。

a) <u>irregular</u> 不規則的

b) <u>pieces</u> 小塊

c) <u>caught</u> 接住

d) <u>never</u> 從來不

e) <u>took his breath away</u> 令他屏息

2. 第五段第三行中的「royal」這個字最接近的意義是

A. 重要的　B. 主要的　C. 貴族的　D. 國王

〔Ans〕 C

3. 第七段第二行中的「privileges」這個字最接近的意義是

A. 好處　B. 珍寶　C. 法律　D. 禮物

〔Ans〕 A

4. 第一段第七行中的「conquered」這個字最接近的意義是

A. 周遊　B. 接管　C. 聯手　D. 來自

〔Ans〕 B

The Moai of Rapa Nui
拉帕努伊的摩艾

Located in Chile（智利）

❶ Rapa Nui is a small island in the middle of the Pacific Ocean. In English, it's known as Easter Island. It's about as far away from everything else as it is possible to be. South America is 3,500 kilometers away, six hours by plane. Nobody arrives at Rapa Nui by accident. Nobody, that is, except the people who arrived there first.

❷ The first people to live on Rapa Nui came from Polynesia.[1] They were far away from home, out exploring the ocean in small boats. When they found land, they decided to stay. In the 12th or 13th century, they began making the giant stone statues, called moai, that have made Rapa Nui famous.

❸ The average moai is four meters tall and weighs 14 tons. Some are more than twice that big. Nearly all of the moai were carved at the same place, in the crater[2] of an extinct[3] volcano called Rano Raraku. Teams of five or six men probably spent

Ⓦ Ⓞ Ⓡ Ⓓ Ⓛ Ⓘ Ⓢ Ⓣ ────────────

1. Polynesia〔ˌpɑləˋniʃə〕 *n.* 玻里尼西亞（大平洋中西部諸小島的總稱）
2. crater〔ˋkretɚ〕 *n.* 噴火口
3. extinct〔ɪkˋstɪŋkt〕 *adj.* 已熄滅的；滅絕的
4. islander〔ˋaɪləndɚ〕 *n.* 島上居民
5. inwards〔ˋɪnwɚdz〕 *adv.* 向內側地
6. geometry〔dʒiˋɑmətrɪ〕 *n.* 幾何學
7. stark〔stɑrk〕 *adj.* 光禿的；荒涼的

about a year on each moai, working the soft volcanic rock with hard rock tools. There are nearly 900 moai on Rapa Nui.

❹ Each moai represented a dead Rapanui leader. The statues were a way for the living to maintain contact with their dead ancestors. In exchange for offerings to the moai, the islanders[4] hoped the ancestors would take good care of them and provide a good life. Most of the erected moai were originally located along the coast of the island. They faced inwards[5] to watch over and protect the people of Rapa Nui.

❺ Almost all the moai are carved in the same style. The geometry[6] of a moai face is stark,[7] angular,[8] and susceptible[9] to dramatic shadows. Moai have long noses and long ears, deep-set eyes, and tightly closed lips that almost seem to be pouting.[10] Originally, they had white coral[11] eyes with red or black pupils.[12] Some wore a kind of cap made from red rock. Moai heads are too big for their bodies. Proportionally,[13] a moai is built

8. angular〔ˋæŋgjələ〕*adj.* 有稜角的
9. susceptible〔səˋsɛptəbḷ〕*adj.* 容易感受……；易受……影響
10. pout〔paʊt〕*v.* 噘嘴
11. coral〔ˋkɔrəl〕*adj.* 珊瑚製的；珊瑚色的
12. pupil〔ˋpjupḷ〕*n.* 瞳孔
13. proportionally〔prəˋpɔrʃənḷɪ〕*adv.* 依比例而定地；相稱地

about like Bart Simpson.

6 These days, moai are famous all around the world. Even people who know nothing about Rapa Nui can recognize a moai. The moai wouldn't have the universal appeal that they do if they didn't look so cool—so elegant, playful,[14] majestic,[15] and mysterious. Somehow a moai manages to look simultaneously[16] primitive and modern, wise and goofy.[17] The charm of the moai can be summarized like this: you feel that if one were to come to life, he would make an excellent friend.

W O R D L I S T

14. playful〔`plefəl〕*adj.* 好玩的
15. majestic〔mə`dʒɛstɪk〕*adj.* 堂皇的；雄偉的
16. simultaneously〔ˌsaɪml̩`tenɪəslɪ〕*adv.* 同時地
17. goofy〔`gufɪ〕*adj.*【俚】笨的；愚蠢的

譯文

❶ 拉帕努伊是太平洋中間的一個小島。在英文裡，它被稱為復活島。它離其他地方差不多是要多遠就有多遠。離南美有 3,500 公里，搭飛機要六小時。沒有人是因為意外而來到拉帕努伊。確實沒有人，除了第一批來到這裡的人。

❷ 第一批住在拉帕努伊的人是來自玻里尼西亞。他們遠離家園，乘著小船出外探索海洋。當他們發現這座島時，便決定待下來。在 12 或 13 世紀時，他們開始建造名為摩艾的巨大石像，並使拉帕努伊因此成名。

❸ 摩艾平均有 4 公尺高、14 噸重，有些則超過兩倍大。所有的摩艾幾乎都是在同一個地方雕刻；在一座名叫拉諾拉拉庫的死火山的火山口。由五、六人所組成的各個隊伍大概一年可做出一具摩艾，他們用堅硬的石具來敲擊鬆軟的火山岩。拉帕努伊將近有 900 具摩艾。

❹ 每具摩艾各代表一位過世的拉帕努伊領袖。雕像是一種讓生者和過世的先人保持聯繫的方式。以供奉摩艾作為交換，島上的居民希望先人能好好照顧他們，並賜予美好的生活。所樹立的摩艾原本大部分位在島的沿岸。它們面向島內，以看管及保護拉帕努伊的居民。

❺ 幾乎所有的摩艾都是雕成同一種樣式。摩艾臉部的幾何圖案是光禿的、有稜有角，並容易形成醒目的陰影。摩艾有長鼻、長耳、深陷的眼睛，緊閉的嘴唇看起來幾乎是噘起來的。原本它們有著白色的珊瑚眼，以及紅色或黑色的瞳孔。有些則戴著一種用紅岩做成的帽子。從它們的體型來看，摩艾的頭顯得過大。依比例來說，摩艾做得有如霸子・辛普森。

❻ 近來摩艾可說是舉世聞名。連對拉帕努伊一無所知的人都能認出摩艾。要是長相沒這麼酷,以及這麼地優雅、討喜、雄偉與神秘,摩艾就不會受到如此廣泛的矚目。不知道怎麼地,摩艾總是看起來既原始又現代,既聰明又傻氣。摩艾的魅力可以總結如下:你會覺得,假如有一尊能活過來,他會是個很棒的朋友。

精要句型

■ *Nobody* arrives at Rapa Nui by accident. *Nobody*, *that is*, except the people who arrived there first.

沒有人是因為意外而來到拉帕努伊。確實沒有人，除了第一批來到這裡的人。

句型 Nobody does Y. Nobody, that is, except X. 「沒有人做 Y。沒有人，也就是說，除了 X。」

這是種強調的說法，用來表示 X 是前述 Y 的例外。

例句 I'm my own boss and *nobody* tells me what to do. *Nobody*, *that is*, *except* my mama.

我就是自己的老闆，沒有人會叫我做什麼。確實沒有人，除了我老媽。

Nobody knows what it is like to fall 10,000 meters through the sky, land, and live to talk about it. *Nobody*, *that is*, *except* Vesna Vulović, the Serbian flight attendant who did just that on January 26, 1972.

沒有人知道從天上一萬公尺下墜、著地並活著講這件事是什麼樣子。確實沒有人，除了在 1972 年 1 月 26 日做過這件事的塞爾維亞空務員 Vesna Vulović。

詞彙測驗

1. Which sentence in each pair is true?

_____ You have to climb to the top of a volcano to find its crater.

_____ You need to dig deep underground to reach a volcano's crater.

_____ Desert landscapes are often stark.

_____ Britney Spears is usually stark.

_____ Your ancestors were real people.

_____ Only if your children have children will you have ancestors.

2. Use words and phrases from the essay to translate each item from Chinese.

遠離家園　　　_____

看顧　　　　　_____

依比例地　　　_____

超過兩倍大　　_____

同時地　　　　_____

活過來　　　　_____

旅 遊 一 點 通

在去拉帕努伊參觀前，一定要先認識鳥人大賽（Bird Man Competition）。它始於 18 世紀，是拉帕努伊部落挑選領袖的新方法。比賽內容包括偷海鳥的蛋，游過鯊魚出沒的危險水域，以及攀爬 250 公尺高的陡崖，以到達終點線。如果要參觀比賽的地方，可以造訪古老的聖城奧隆戈（Orongo），它就在該島三座火山之一的拉諾考外緣（Rano Kau）。可到下列網站看看，當鳥人冠軍需要什麼條件：

http://chile-travel.suite101.com/article.cfm/easter_island_birdman_competition

旅遊好用句

拉帕努伊有一片海灘可以讓遊客游泳。去不熟悉的海灘游泳前，最好先找當地人問一下情況：

Is it safe to swim here? Are there riptides or anything else I need to worry about?

「在這裡游泳安全嗎？有激流或別的我需要擔心的事嗎？」

詞彙測驗

1. 各組中的哪句話寫得才正確？

　T　 你必須爬到火山頂，才能找到它的火山口。

＿＿＿ 你要往地下挖得很深，才能到達火山的火山口。

　T　 沙漠的景象多半是光禿荒涼的。

＿＿＿ 小甜甜布蘭妮通常是光禿的。

　T　 先人是真實的人。

＿＿＿ 只有當你的子女有小孩時，你們才會有先人。

2. 利用文中的單字及片語來譯出各個中文片語。

- far away from home
- watch over
- proportionally
- more than twice that big
- simultaneously
- come to life

UNIT 21 | **Christ the Redeemer**
救世基督像

Located in Brazil（巴西）

❶ Christ the Redeemer[1] is a statue that stands on top of Corcovado Mountain in the center of Rio de Janeiro, Brazil. Made of concrete and soapstone,[2] forty meters tall on its pedestal,[3] the statue shows Jesus with outstretched[4] arms. He seems to be reaching out to embrace the city spread out below.

❷ The statue's posture is a reminder of how Jesus died. Christians believe that Jesus was the son of God and that he died so that men would be forgiven and escape punishment for their sins. They believe Jesus died to redeem[5] us.

❸ From the edge of a 700-meter cliff, Christ the Redeemer overlooks[6] a spectacular panorama[7] of green mountains, white buildings, and blue sea. Some visitors say the view from Corcovado is the most beautiful thing they have ever seen.

❹ Millions of people live in Rio de Janeiro. A few are incredibly rich. A far greater number are very poor. The dramatic contrast between the rich and poor neighborhoods is clearly visible from the top of

---

Ⓦⓞⓡⓓ Ⓛⓘⓢⓣ

1. Redeemer 〔rɪˋdimɚ〕 *n.* 贖罪者；救主；基督
2. soapstone 〔ˋsop͵ston〕 *n.* 皂石
3. pedestal 〔ˋpɛdɪstl〕 *n.* 基座；台
4. outstretched 〔autˋstrɛtʃt〕 *adj.* 張開的；伸長的
5. redeem 〔rɪˋdim〕 *v.* 救贖；償還
6. overlook 〔͵ovɚˋluk〕 *v.* 俯瞰

Corcovado Mountain. The rich live along Rio's white sand beaches in neighborhoods like Ipanema and Leblon. The poor live in hillside[8] slums[9] called *favelas*—places like Rocinha and Jacarezinho.

❺ What is happening down there in the city? Everything—every imaginable human thing—is happening. Rio is famous for music, dancing, and a joyful approach to life. The city also has a reputation for robbery, violence, and murder.

❻ Once a year, just before Easter, Rio throws[10] the world's biggest happiest sexiest party—*Carnaval*. Rio is also a city where many *favelas* are controlled by armed gangs,[11] and where about 1,000 people are killed each year—by the police.

❼ Rio is a place where it's easy to meet people who will become your friends for life. It's also a place where doctors know how to repair ears cut in half by kidnappers. Rio is a city where a man dressed as Santa

7. panorama〔͵pænəˋræmə〕 *n.* 全景
8. hillside〔ˋhɪl͵saɪd〕 *n.* 山腰；丘陵的斜面
9. slum〔slʌm〕 *n.* 貧民窟；貧民區
10. throw〔θro〕 *v.* 辦（舞會）；舉行（晚宴）
11. gang〔gæŋ〕 *n.* 黑幫；暴力集團

Claus once flew in a helicopter[12] to deliver Christmas presents to children in a *favela*. People on the ground started shooting at the helicopter. They thought Santa Claus was police. Santa Claus wasn't really all that surprised. He didn't give up. After landing the helicopter, he carried on and delivered the presents in a car.

❽ Up on top of Corcovado Mountain, Christ the Redeemer is well placed to see people shooting at Santa Claus and all the other crazy wonderful lovely evil stuff that happens down in the city. The Redeemer's reaction is always the same: he tilts[13] his head  just slightly towards his left shoulder, a gesture that seems to signal[14] understanding and compassion,[15] and he reaches his arms out to give Rio a big hug.

W O R D   L I S T

12. helicopter〔ˋhɛlɪˌkɑptɚ〕 *n.* 直升機
13. tilt〔tɪlt〕 *v.* 傾斜
14. signal〔ˋsɪgn!〕 *v.* 示意；發信號
15. compassion〔kəmˋpæʃən〕 *n.* 同情；憐憫

譯文

① 救世基督像是樹立在巴西里約熱內盧中央的科爾科瓦杜山上的雕像。用混凝土和滑石所打造，在基座上有 40 公尺高，這座雕像的外型是展開雙臂的耶穌。他似乎張臂擁抱著底下綿延的城市。

② 雕像的姿態會讓人想起耶穌的死因。基督徒相信，耶穌是上帝之子，他的死讓人類的罪愆獲得了寬恕，並免除了責罰。他們相信，耶穌是為了救贖我們而死的。

③ 從 700 公尺高的懸崖邊緣，救世基督像俯瞰著壯觀的全景，包括綠色的高山、白色的建築，以及藍色的大海。有些遊客說，科爾科瓦杜的景色是他們有史以來所看過最美麗的景象。

④ 里約熱內盧住了好幾百萬人。有些極為富有，絕大多數的人則非常貧窮。在科爾科瓦杜山的山頂，貧富地區的強烈對比清晰可見。有錢人住在里約的白色海灘沿線，像是伊帕內馬和萊布隆等地區。窮人則住在半山腰名為 *favela* 的貧民區裡，像是荷欣尼亞和札卡瑞辛尤等地。

⑤ 下面這個城市都在上演些什麼事件？什麼都有，包含一切可以想見的人類大小事。里約是以音樂、舞蹈和歡樂的生活型態而著稱。而市內的搶劫、暴力與謀殺同樣遠近馳名。

⑥ 一年一度，就在復活節前夕，里約會舉辦全世界最盛大、最歡樂、最性感的派對——嘉年華會。里約也是個有許多 *favela* 被武力幫派所掌控的城市，每年大約會有 1,000 人死在警察手裡。

❼ 里約是個很容易跟認識的人變成終生好友的地方。它也是個醫生知道要怎麼把被綁匪切成兩半的耳朵給接好的地方。在里約這個城市，也曾有人扮成聖誕老人搭著直升機發送禮物給 *favela* 的小朋友。在地面上的人卻開始對直升機開槍，他們以為聖誕老人是警察。聖誕老人其實並沒有那麼吃驚，也沒有放棄。直升機降落後，他繼續坐著車子發送禮物。

❽ 在科爾科瓦杜山的山頂，救世基督像被擺在一個視野絕佳的地方，看著民眾對聖誕老人開槍，以及其他一切瘋狂、精彩、美好、惡劣的事在底下的城市上演。救世基督像的反應永遠都一樣：他只是把頭稍稍偏向左肩，一種似乎是在表示理解與同情的姿勢，並張開雙臂給里約一個大大的擁抱。

 **精要句型**

■ Rio *is famous for* music, dancing and a joyful approach to life.
里約是以音樂、舞蹈和歡樂的生活型態而著稱。

句型 **X is famous for Y.**「**X** 是以 **Y** 而著稱。」

類似句型有：has a reputation for、is known for。

例句 Puli *is famous for* its four Ws: water, wine, women, and weather.
埔里是以四個 W 而著稱：水、酒、美女和天氣。

Luke *was famous for* eating fifty hardboiled eggs in one hour.
路克是以一個小時能吃 50 顆水煮蛋而著稱。

 **詞彙測驗**

Match the words from the box to the speakers.

compassion	slum	robbery	murder	present

_____ **1.** When it comes to drug dealers, I say shoot first and ask questions later. Call it what you want. I call it justice.

_____ **2.** More than 100,000 people are packed into one square kilometer. Some have running water, some don't. There are no schools. It's a really friendly place, but it can also be dangerous. Don't go without a guide.

_____ **3.** They took everything: camera, credit cards, even my shoes! They plucked me like a chicken!

_____ **4.** Why can't you try for once to understand how I feel? Put yourself in my shoes. Other people do have feelings—did you know that?

_____ **5.** Is that for me? What is it? No—you didn't. You did not. You did? Oh—My—God! You did!

旅 遊 一 點 通

里約流行一種非常小件的比基尼叫做 fio dental，也就是牙線的意思。世界上最性感的海灘有些就在里約，很多人想去。海灘上擠滿了本地人和遊客——還有小偷。如果要防堵小偷，第一步就是不要穿得像遊客，而要穿得像本地人。不要戴名貴的錶。不要猛看旅遊指南。把相機藏在便宜的塑膠袋裡。你或許沒辦法完全融入，但起碼可以避免引人側目而成為明顯的目標。里約海灘的資料及安全須知可到下列網站查詢：

http://www.braziltravelvacation.com/brazil-beaches.html

旅遊好用句

第二步則是盡可能多了解當地的狀況，多多發問：

Is it safe to go jogging on this beach early in the morning?
「一大早在這片海灘上慢跑安不安全？」

詞彙測驗

把框框裡的單字跟說話者配對。

1. murder

譯文 談到毒販，我認為要先開槍再問問題。隨你要怎麼形容，我說這叫做正義。

2. slum

譯文 一平方公里內擠了超過 10 萬人。有些人有自來水可用，有些人沒有。沒有學校。那是個相當親切的地方，但也可能很危險。沒有嚮導可別去。

3. robbery

譯文 他們什麼都拿：相機、信用卡，甚至是我的鞋子！他們把我像小孩一樣拉扯！

4. compassion

譯文 你為什麼不能就這一次試著去了解我有什麼感覺？你站在我的立場想一想。別人可是會有感覺的——你明白這點嗎？

5. present

譯文 那是給我的嗎？什麼東西？不會吧——你沒買，你沒有買吧。你買了？喔，天哪！你買了！

圖片來源

Unit 1：
http://commons.wikimedia.org/wiki/File:Sphinx_und_Chephren-Pyramide.jpg
http://commons.wikimedia.org/wiki/File:The_First_and_Last_Wonder.jpg
http://commons.wikimedia.org/wiki/File:Chambre-roi-grande-pyramide.jpg
http://commons.wikimedia.org/wiki/File:Egyptian_mummy_(Louvre).JPG

Unit 2：
http://commons.wikimedia.org/wiki/File:Petra_Treasury.jpg
http://commons.wikimedia.org/wiki/File:Petra_Treasury_Urn.jpg
http://commons.wikimedia.org/wiki/File:CamelsPetra.jpg
http://commons.wikimedia.org/wiki/File:Petra_Monastary_Framed.jpg
http://commons.wikimedia.org/wiki/File:Petra_Monastary.jpg
http://commons.wikimedia.org/wiki/File:Siq14(js).jpg

Unit 3：
http://commons.wikimedia.org/wiki/File:Djingareiber_cour.jpg
http://commons.wikimedia.org/wiki/File:Medersa_Sankore.jpg
http://commons.wikimedia.org/wiki/File:Sankore_Mosque_in_Timbuktu.jpg
http://commons.wikimedia.org/wiki/File:Sankore_Moske_Timboektoe.JPG
http://commons.wikimedia.org/wiki/File:1997_270A-24_Niger_River.jpg

Unit 4：
http://commons.wikimedia.org/wiki/File:Kiyomizu-dera_in_Kyoto.jpg
http://commons.wikimedia.org/wiki/File:Otowa_waterfall_at_Kiyomizu-dera.jpg
http://commons.wikimedia.org/wiki/File:Kiyomizu-dera_beams1.JPG

Unit 5：
http://commons.wikimedia.org/wiki/File:Buddhist_monks_in_front_of_the_Angkor_Wat.jpg
黃丹萬

Unit 6：
http://commons.wikimedia.org/wiki/File:The_Great_Wall_pic_1.jpg

http://commons.wikimedia.org/wiki/File:The_Great_Wall_of_China_in_sand.JPG
http://commons.wikimedia.org/wiki/File:Great_Wall_detail.jpg
http://upload.wikimedia.org/wikipedia/commons/archive/c/c8/20070311032915%21Great_Wall_unrestored_Guard_Tower.jpg
http://commons.wikimedia.org/wiki/File:Shanhaiguan_great_wall.jpg

Unit 7：
http://commons.wikimedia.org/wiki/File:StBasile_SpasskayaTower_Red_Square_Moscow.hires.jpg
http://commons.wikimedia.org/wiki/File:Moscow_-_Entrance_of_Red_Square.jpg
http://commons.wikimedia.org/wiki/File:Moscow_State_Historical_Museum_Red_Square.jpg
http://commons.wikimedia.org/wiki/File:Moscow_-_Saint_Basil%27s_Cathedral.jpg
http://commons.wikimedia.org/wiki/File:Lenin%27s_Tomb.jpg
http://commons.wikimedia.org/wiki/File:HaKremlin_IMG_6795.JPG

Unit 8：
http://commons.wikimedia.org/wiki/File:Hagia_Sophia_09.JPG
http://commons.wikimedia.org/wiki/File:Haga_Sofia_RB3.jpg
http://commons.wikimedia.org/wiki/File:574IstanbulSSofia.JPG
http://commons.wikimedia.org/wiki/File:Haga_Sofia_NMP_RB1.jpg

Unit 9：
http://commons.wikimedia.org/wiki/File:Wonder_of_the_World_-_The_Taj_Mahal_(1630_A.D.)_Agra,_India.jpg
http://commons.wikimedia.org/wiki/File:Arches_in_the_Taj_Mahal_Mosque_interior,_Agra.jpg
http://commons.wikimedia.org/wiki/File:B9a_agra700.jpg
http://commons.wikimedia.org/wiki/File:Taj_6_agost_05.jpg

Unit 10：
http://commons.wikimedia.org/wiki/File:1_The_Opera_House_in_Sydney.jpg
http://commons.wikimedia.org/wiki/File:Sydney_Opera_House_Sails_edit02.jpg
http://commons.wikimedia.org/wiki/File:Sydney_Opera_House_-_Up_Close_at_night.jpg
http://commons.wikimedia.org/wiki/File:Sydney_Opera_House_with_Tall_Ship.jpg

Unit 11：
http://commons.wikimedia.org/wiki/File:Colosseum_in_Rome-

April_2007-1-_copie_2B.jpg
http://commons.wikimedia.org/wiki/File:Colosseum_Rome.jpg
http://commons.wikimedia.org/wiki/File:Colosseum3_11-7-2003.
JPG

Unit 12 :
http://commons.wikimedia.org/wiki/File:Lightmatter_acropolis.jpg
http://commons.wikimedia.org/wiki/File:Parthenon.jpg
http://commons.wikimedia.org/wiki/File:Parthenon_-_facade_est.
jpg
http://commons.wikimedia.org/wiki/File:South_metope_27_
Parthenon_BM.jpg
http://commons.wikimedia.org/wiki/File:East_pediment_E_
Parthenon_BM.jpg

Unit 13 :
http://commons.wikimedia.org/wiki/File:Alhambra_vista_desde_
San_Nicolas.jpg
http://commons.wikimedia.org/wiki/File:80525560_0eb2c1d54a_
o.jpg
http://commons.wikimedia.org/wiki/File:Granada_Alhambra_
Fuente_de_los_leones.jpg
http://commons.wikimedia.org/wiki/File:Alhambra-Granada-Sala_
de_las_dos_Hermanas.jpg
http://commons.wikimedia.org/wiki/File:Alhambra_Garden.JPG
http://commons.wikimedia.org/wiki/File:Devise_Nasride_1.jpg

Unit 14 :
http://commons.wikimedia.org/wiki/File:Eiffel_tower.jpg
http://commons.wikimedia.org/wiki/File:From_Below.jpg
http://commons.wikimedia.org/wiki/File:Eiffel_Tower_Restaurant_
in_Las_Vegas.JPG

Unit 15 :
http://commons.wikimedia.org/wiki/File:Zamek_
Neuschwanstein_09.jpg
http://commons.wikimedia.org/wiki/File:Neuschwanstein_Boden.
jpg
http://commons.wikimedia.org/wiki/File:Neuschwanstein_Gang.jpg
http://commons.wikimedia.org/wiki/File:Zamek_
Neuschwanstein_01.jpg

Unit 16 :
http://commons.wikimedia.org/wiki/File:Stonehenge-England.jpg
http://commons.wikimedia.org/wiki/File:Stonehenge_Inside_
Facing_NE_April_2005.jpg

http://commons.wikimedia.org/wiki/File:Stonehenge_sun_through_
trilith_April_2005.jpg

Unit 17 :
http://commons.wikimedia.org/wiki/File:Chitzen_Itze.JPG
http://commons.wikimedia.org/wiki/File:Chichen-Itza-Great-Ball-
Court.jpg
http://commons.wikimedia.org/wiki/File:GreatBallCourt.jpg

Unit 18 :
http://commons.wikimedia.org/wiki/File:Liberty-statue-from-front.
jpg
http://commons.wikimedia.org/wiki/File:Statue_of_Liberty_
frontal_2.jpg
http://commons.wikimedia.org/wiki/File:ToesMissLiberty.jpg
http://commons.wikimedia.org/wiki/File:Liberty-statue-with-
manhattan.jpg

Unit 19 :
http://commons.wikimedia.org/wiki/File:MachuPichuSacredValley_
fir000202_edit.jpg
http://commons.wikimedia.org/wiki/File:Machu_picchu_grande.jpg
http://commons.wikimedia.org/wiki/File:Peru_Machu_Picchu_
Sunrise.jpg
http://commons.wikimedia.org/wiki/File:Machu-picchu-c17.jpg
http://commons.wikimedia.org/wiki/File:Machu-picchu-c19.jpg

Unit 20 :
http://commons.wikimedia.org/wiki/File:Ahu_Tongariki_-_Rapa_
Nui_(Easter_Island).JPG
http://commons.wikimedia.org/wiki/File:Moai_Easter_Island_
InvMH-35-61-1.jpg
http://commons.wikimedia.org/wiki/File:AhuTongariki.JPG

Unit 21 :
http://commons.wikimedia.org/wiki/File:Christ_on_Corcovado_
mountain.JPG
http://commons.wikimedia.org/wiki/File:Cristo_Redentor_Rio_de_
Janeiro_2.jpg
http://commons.wikimedia.org/wiki/File:Christ_the_Redeemer.jpg
http://commons.wikimedia.org/wiki/File:Leszek_Wasilewski-
rocinha.jpg

國家圖書館出版品預行編目資料

英文閱讀越好：旅遊篇 / Jeff Hammons 作；戴至中譯. －－ 初版.
－－ 臺北市：貝塔出版：智勝文化發行, 2010. 04
　　面；　公分
　　ISBN　978-957-729-781-5（平裝附光碟片）

　1. 英語　2. 旅遊　3. 讀本

805.18　　　　　　　　　　　　　　　　　　99003770

英文閱讀越好：旅遊篇

作　　者 / Jeff Hammons
譯　　者 / 戴至中
執行編輯 / 陳家仁

出　　版 / 貝塔出版有限公司
地　　址 / 台北市 100 館前路 12 號 11 樓
電　　話 / (02) 2314-2525
傳　　真 / (02) 2312-3535
客服專線 / (02) 2314-3535
客服信箱 / btservice@betamedia.com.tw
郵撥帳號 / 19493777
帳戶名稱 / 貝塔出版有限公司

總 經 銷 / 時報文化出版企業股份有限公司
地　　址 / 桃園縣龜山鄉萬壽路二段 351 號
電　　話 / (02) 2306-6842

出版日期 / 2010 年 04 月初版一刷
定　　價 / 280 元
ISBN ： 978-957-729-781-5

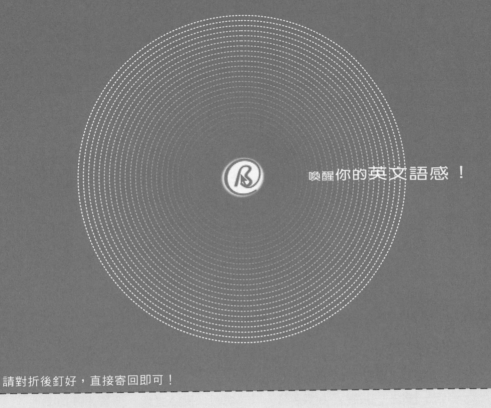

喚醒你的英文語感！

請對折後釘好，直接寄回即可！

100 台北市中正區館前路12號11樓

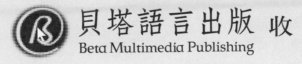 貝塔語言出版 收
Beta Multimedia Publishing

 寄件者住址 □ □ □

貝塔語言出版
Beta Multimedia Publishing

讀者服務專線 (02) 2314-3535 讀者服務傳真 (02) 2312-3535
客戶服務信箱 btservice@betamedia.com.tw
www.betamedia.com.tw

謝謝您購買本書！！

貝塔語言擁有最優良之英文學習書籍，為提供您最佳的英語學習資訊，您填妥此表後寄回（免貼郵票），將可不定期免費收到本公司最新發行之書訊及活動訊息！

姓名：＿＿＿＿＿＿＿＿＿＿　性別：☐男 ☐女　生日：＿＿年＿＿月＿＿日

電話：（公）＿＿＿＿＿＿＿（宅）＿＿＿＿＿＿＿（手機）＿＿＿＿＿＿＿

電子信箱：＿＿＿＿＿＿＿＿＿＿＿＿＿＿＿＿＿＿＿＿＿＿＿＿＿

學歷：☐高中職含以下　☐專科　☐大學　☐研究所含以上

職業：☐金融 ☐服務 ☐傳播 ☐製造 ☐資訊 ☐軍公教 ☐出版
　　　☐自由 ☐教育 ☐學生 ☐其他

職級：☐企業負責人　☐高階主管　☐中階主管　☐職員　☐專業人士

1. 您購買的書籍是？＿＿＿＿＿＿＿＿＿＿＿＿＿＿＿＿＿＿＿＿

2. 您從何處得知本產品？（可複選）

☐書店 ☐網路 ☐書展 ☐校園活動 ☐廣告信函 ☐他人推薦 ☐新聞報導 ☐其他＿＿

3. 您覺得本產品價格：

☐偏高 ☐合理 ☐偏低

4. 請問目前您每週花了多少時間學英語？

☐不到十分鐘 ☐十分鐘以上，但不到半小時 ☐半小時以上，但不到一小時
☐一小時以上，但不到兩小時 ☐兩個小時以上 ☐不一定

5. 通常在選擇語言學習書時，哪些因素是您會考慮的？

☐封面 ☐內容、實用性 ☐品牌 ☐媒體、朋友推薦 ☐價格 ☐其他＿＿＿

6. 市面上您最需要的語言書種類為？

☐聽力 ☐閱讀 ☐文法 ☐口說 ☐寫作 ☐其他＿＿＿

7. 通常您會透過何種方式選購語言學習書籍？

☐書店門市 ☐網路書店 ☐郵購 ☐直接找出版社 ☐學校或公司團購 ☐其他＿＿

8. 給我們的建議：＿＿＿＿＿＿＿＿＿＿＿＿＿＿＿＿＿＿＿＿

＿＿＿＿＿＿＿＿＿＿＿＿＿＿＿＿＿＿＿＿＿＿＿＿＿＿＿＿＿

＿＿＿＿＿＿＿＿＿＿＿＿＿＿＿＿＿＿＿＿＿＿＿＿＿＿＿＿＿

喚醒你的英文語感！

Get a Feel for English !

喚醒你的英文語感！

Get a Feel for English !